RON KRAMER
MUSIC BOX

PANDA BOOKS PRESS

ISBN: 978-0-692-78668-0

Copyright © 2016 by Panda Press Books LLC
All rights reserved.

No part of this publication may be reproduced, distributed, or transmitted in any form or by any means, including information storage and retrieval systems, photocopying, recording, or other electronic or mechanical methods, without the prior written permission of the author, except in the case of brief quotations embodied in critical reviews and certain other noncommercial uses permitted by copyright law.
This book is a work of fiction. Names, characters, places, and incidents either are products of the author's imagination or are used fictitiously.
Any resemblance to actual persons, living or dead, events, or locales is entirely coincidental.
For permission requests, email the publisher at: PR@pandabookspress.com

Dedication

For my dear mother Elfriede, your love and kindness
was the inspiration for this magical story.

Dec. 13, 1939
Aug. 29, 1996

You are forever in my heart.

Table of Contents

The Library	1
Together as one	5
Adalwolf and the Shadows	13
Shall we dance	17
A day to remember	19
Panic in the village	23
Elfriede meets Teodora	27
The Journey	33
The Message is received	37
The Gardens of Belvedere	41
The Awakening of General Kristof	45
Prisoner Eugene	47
United	49
Dinner for Two	53
The Silver Storm	57
Battle of Swords	65
The Waltz and Ending	77
A Familiar Voice	85

The Library

It was that time of year again, summer vacation. And like the previous year, I found myself sitting out by the lake at my grandparents' summer home in upstate Connecticut. The flowers in my grandmother's rock garden were vibrant like the year before and emitted the most wonderful fragrance you could have hoped for. As I gazed upon the lake, I could still remember that hot Fourth of July when I learned how to swim for the first time. Oh…how rude of me I forgot to introduce myself, my name is Hieke.

I flipped my long blonde hair over my shoulder as I glanced over at my grandmother, and as usual she was tending to my grandfather. My Opa was never short for words when he wanted something. He would call out to my Oma in his soft but demanding voice, "Schatzi, can you please bring over the lemonade?"

I couldn't help but laugh a little as my Oma would rush over to him before he had enough time to repeat his order.

Across the lake was a young family with two children, Margarete and Honnalore. They were about the same age as me and we spent many days playing together at the lake in summers past. "Schatzi….Schatzi!" Now it was my Oma calling me. "Your friends are back again this summer."

"Yes, I know."

"Why don't you take the boat over and see if they want to have dinner with us later?"

"Not right now, Oma," I said. "Actually, I was thinking of going inside for a bit."

"Inside, dear? Why?"

"Yes, I want to find a new book to read for the summer."

She paused for a moment and then rolled her eyes. "Oh. Ok, dear, but don't stay in there all day, you just got here and we have so much to talk about."

"Ok, Oma. I promise."

I handed my empty glass of lemonade to her and slowly made my way up the back porch and into the house. The excitement started to build as I continued toward my favorite room, the library. It wasn't an ordinary library -- it was a wondrous library. My favorite place to spend my days when I visited, and even more interesting than playing down at the lake with my summertime friends. As I entered the room, I quickly turned on the lights and paused. After a few seconds the antique style lamps flickered and came to a cheerful glow. "Wow!" I whispered to myself as I made my way in. There were no windows in my grandparents' library, just shelves upon shelves of books tucked into every nook and cranny. The many shapes and unique book covers always fascinated me. I usually would pick out one simply because of its cover and how enchanting it looked. So today was the first day of summer vacation and I was hungry for a new adventure. Under my feet I could hear the wooden floorboards creaking beneath my weight as I continued to walk in and gaze up and down the walls looking for my next treasure. An eerie feeling washed over me...did I? I swore that I heard a faint melody in the distance. I stood silently straining my ears. It must have been my imagination I thought to myself. Glancing around I studied the covers on each bookshelf trying to decide which book would be the one. Then I heard it again, it was very faint but I knew for certain that it was no longer my imagination.

I tilted my head, honing my ears in on the ghostly noise, slowly I inched myself forward, I could feel my heart pounding in my chest. With each step the sound became more audible, once I could make out the melody, my pulse steadied, it was very relaxing. The tune was intoxicating, I found myself humming it out loud and rhythmically fell into dance like a ballerina.

Looking straight ahead, I noticed my favorite nook in the library and then the music stopped just as quickly as it had started. It was a window seat located in the far end of the room but without the window. An area just big enough for me to climb up into that was soft with a thick cushion for me to lay down on. Surrounding this cubbyhole were some smaller shelves filled with books and a few antiques my Oma would collect in her travels over the years. Then it caught my eye. "What's this?" Used as one of the bookends, sat a beautiful music box. "Hmmm, this wasn't here last year." I reached over, picked it up and held it gently. My Oma had recently visited Germany this past year and I'm sure that is where she found this marvelous antique. It was so beautiful, handcrafted in wood and encrusted with colorful jewels. I opened the top lid and listened. Sure enough, a sweet blend of music emitted from the inside, it was the same timeless melody I heard. It sent a chill down my spine. The tune was so beautiful yet haunting at the same time. Suddenly I began to feel a warm sensation that tingled up and down my body as I continued to hold the music box. This felt strange to me and made me a little nervous. So I quickly returned the music box onto the shelf making sure it went back in the same place where it had been holding up the other books.

In haste, I knocked over one of the books, I tried to catch it but it tumbled off the shelf and came straight down onto my lap. It was an old book, worn out with a brown leather cover and gold lettering on the front. I turned it over to read the title before returning it to the shelf. I could faintly make out the gold embossed lettering. It simply read, "Music Box." Hmmmm. Ok, maybe this belonged with the music box it sat next to. I decided to open it up and glance inside. Remarkably, the pages were old and yellow but very readable, not like the outside cover. This gained my attention as I sat back and decided to explore this a little further, I grab my favorite blanket and draped it over my shoulders. Then I adjusted the lamp above for a little extra light, I swore the pages had a faint glow about them, but maybe it was from the lamp, I started reading the opening chapter...

Together as one

Close your eyes and dream....

In a small village deep in the Black Forest of Germany, lived a young eight-year-old girl and her mother, and father. The small town was bordered by large, green, rolling mountains that scraped the skies above and dense forest with tall pine, spruce, beech, and oak trees. They were middle class and had a fair amount of material possessions, but what they treasured most were each other. Gustav was a kind and loving father who loved to sing and dance. He also was the best baker and bread maker in town. His wife Hilde, was a very creative and talented dressmaker. Her dresses were sought after by many ladies of class, even a few princesses from far away kingdoms, requested her to make them dresses for their special day from time to time. Then there was their daughter Elfriede, she was young and beautiful, but also shy and whimsical. She would often drift away and dance to her own stories as she worked alongside her father selling bread in the streets of the village, wearing one of the many beautiful dresses her mother made for her. Elfriede enjoyed a special bond with her parent's. They all shared the same love of music and dance, and for Elfriede, her family was everything in the world to her. They would often dance together, especially at the town festivities every weekend.

Elfriede loved dancing with her parents' at festivals, but she also secretly looked forward to seeing her best friend Eugen, he was a year older than her. They often got lost in dance and found themselves alone and away from everyone else. They spent every free moment together when they got a chance. When they were together, they liked that they felt comfortable enough to be themselves. They both had overactive imaginations and would come up with lots of silly games, where they would dance around pretending to slay mythical creatures such as dragons, and other times Eugene would pretend that he was a brave knight rescuing her from whatever situation they dreamed up.

***

Elfriede was overly excited, it was time for her family to go to the festival and she had a marvelous idea. She came up with a new game for Eugene and herself to play today. She routinely put her hair back in a ponytail as she got ready, twirling around in a circle just fast enough to lift her flowing, yellow dress.

Elfriede stopped dead in her tracks. "Momma!" She exclaimed.

She rushed to her mother's side, knelt down and shook her. "Momma please wake up." She pouted.

"Papa, come quickly its Momma, she's sick."

Gustav rushed into the room, and saw his wife collapsed on the kitchen floor. "Elfriede fetch me a pale of water, quickly child."

Elfriede did as instructed, and then stood trembling with fear as she watched her father feverishly work over her mother. After a while he scooped up his wife and put her to bed.

"Will momma be OK?"

Gustav tugged at his mustache, "Its fever. If it doesn't show any sign of improvement by morning, I'll send for a doctor."

Elfriede collapsed by her mother's bedside and pouted until she fell asleep. The next morning, she woke up to the sound of a strangers' voice, it was a doctor from the next town over. The words she won't make it through the week burned into her ears. This had to be a nightmare she thought to herself. But slowly reality dug deeply into her, as her mother's health faded with each passing day. Elfriede and Gustav cared for her day and night, taking shifts as the fever slowly took her from them

On the final day, Hilde woke from her deep sleep. She reached her hand down and ran her fingers through her daughter's soft hair. "Elfriede wake, wake my sweet girl."

Elfriede sprung up from the floor in disbelief. "Father, Father come quick. Mother woken!"

Gustav dashed to his wife's side, he paused to study her. Elfriede noted the concern in her father's eyes.

Hilde ratcheted her eyes onto Gustavs' and then onto Elfriede's. "I am so sorry, is it selfish of me to pass?" She said, tears streaming down her face.

Gustav took his wife's hands and held them gently, looking deep into her soul. "You did not ask for this, none of us did. If you must go, we will be fine. Do not hold on for us my sweet, sweet wife."

Hilde took a deep breath, struggling to force out her last wishes. "Dance for me, we never made it to the festival. She took another deep breath focusing her gaze on Elfriede, "Momma will always be with you my angel, whenever you miss me dance with your Papa and I will be dancing alongside you, when you dance together."

Gustav and Elfriede danced together as Hilde watched and smiled, after their dance she drifted off into an eternal slumber, leaving them both behind.

Elfriede strayed away from the village after her Momma's passing. No matter how hard Gustav pleaded with her to come into the village and work with him, she would not budge. She also refused to dance with her Father on the weekends, and he would go alone to honor his wife's memory. She had too many great memories of her Momma and them dancing together there, this was such a happy place for her family that she did not want to taint her memories. She wanted to only remember all the fun she had there with her Momma and she feared if she returned to the village these memories would fade, and new memories would replace the old.

Eight years later, on the eve of Elfriede's sixteenth birthday, Gustav knew he wanted to surprise his daughter with something special, unlike anything he had ever given her before. Gustav was now poor due to his wife passing and had little money to spend He had heard word from the local townsfolk that a band of gypsies lived deep in the Fern Blackwood's and they accepted barter. Gustav filled his pouch with every cent he owned and a few family heirlooms, he was determined to make this day special for his daughter.

Once deep enough in the forest, Gustav stumbled upon a mysterious gypsy. Mysterious because she seemed to materialize from nowhere from the depths of the forest shadows. Dressed in typical and colorful gypsy attire complete with head scarf, she approached him quite aggressively. Startled, Gustav was taken back but soon regained his composure. He spoke up right away and said, "I need something special for my daughter's birthday."

In a raspy voice the gypsy hissed, "I have the most beautiful gifts your daughter could ever ask for!" Without hesitation the mysterious gypsy produced a colorful scarf. Gustav frowned, saying, "My daughter already has a scarf."

She then reached into her bag a second time and pulled out a lovely hat. Again the disappointed father shook his head, saying, "No, my daughter already has a red hat with white feathers that I gave her last year. I want to give her something very special because this year will be her sixteenth birthday."

So the mysterious gypsy paused for a moment and looked behind her and then behind Gustav, seemingly to ascertain they were alone. She knelt on the ground and started to dig deep into her sack of trinkets. The strange lady hesitated at first and looked back once more before she pulled out a beautiful music box carved out of wood and decorated with gold trim. As soon as Gustav laid his eyes on the music box he shouted, "That's it! That's the perfect gift! I'm sure she will be delighted!"

The gypsy smiled. "Yes it is indeed. This music box captures the heart and spirit of any young girl who believes in love, music and dance."

Then her face darkened and her voice lowered. "But be warned, it comes with a price, a price most anyone would not want to pay."

Gustav fixed his resolute eyes upon her. "Whatever the price is I will pay! I know Elfriede will cherish this for sure. She loves music, she loves to dance, it's perfect!"

Gustav reached into his pouch to pay the gypsy he would offer her all of the coins he'd brought with him.

The gypsy let out an eerie laugh. "It is not you who must pay."

Before he could turn back around to say another word the gypsy had vanished! Thinking this was strange for a moment, he noticed the music box sitting on the ground, in the place the gypsy was previously standing. Gustav waited for a while to make sure the gypsy didn't change her mind. After waiting a bit, he decided to head back home. He spun around in a mixture of excitement and confusion making his journey back to the village hoping to make it before nightfall. He could hardly wait to give Elfriede her special birthday gift.

The following morning, the village prepared for its weekend festivities and dance. This was a time Elfriede and her dad used to treasure. Gustav was determined to bring his daughter to the village for her birthday. With his mind set on that he approached her with confidence. "Daughter it has been eight long years since you been to work with me. I miss us dancing and spending that time together. Gustav lowered his head appearing sad. "Please come with me on this special day, I have the most wonderful gift for you."

Elfriede blew a long strand of hair out of her eyes. "I will consider it."

Elfriede was curious what gift her father had got her, she was sure it be wonderful. She used to enjoy coming up with new and creative dance routines to show off and dazzle the village folks every weekend, so she decided that she too would give her father a special gift this day.

Elfriede was as excited as she was happy, she just told her father that she would go into the village with him. She had prepared a lovely dance to be shared with her beloved father on this special day, they danced together every day, but today they would dance together in public like old times. As they both traveled to town, Elfriede would teach and show her dad all the new dance steps that she had planned for later in the day. Once they arrived, they began to set up the food cart to sell all their delicious breads and pastries that Gustav had prepared.

It was a busy morning as they worked together and Elfriede's elation grew, thinking of the birthday gift her dad would give her. Finally, Gustav turned to his daughter and said, "Happy Birthday my dear," and he took out a beautifully wrapped present.

Elfriede's eyes widened and glowed. As she unwrapped her gift she grew more and more titillated with the anticipation. At last, it was unwrapped. "Oh my, a music box." She turned it around and around and hesitated to open the lid. "I love it, Father, it's beautiful!"

Gustav, his chest pumped up said, "You're welcome, dear, but you must open it to hear the lovely music from within." Elfriede then carefully opened the lid and was quickly enraptured by the haunting angelic music, which was accompanied by a flash of light and a warm glow that came from inside. I love it, Father. I love it! I've never heard anything like this before, it's so beautiful!"

She then put down the music box but left the lid open and began to dance, the dance routine that she had worked on all week. It fit perfectly, every note and every melody joined her and the music together as one into a perfectly choreographed piece. "Come on, Father," she called, "shall we dance?"

Elfriede bowed low in curtsey holding on to both sides of her dress as Gustav held out his hand and said, "It would be my honor to share this dance with you."

Together they danced around the town square capturing the attention of everyone.

"This new dance is wonderful" Gustav said as he gracefully spun his daughter. "I can feel your Momma dancing with us."

A young man also worked in the village square. He sold flowers from his cart with his mother, Ingeborg. He watched the dancing duo and couldn't take his eyes off of Elfriede. He never saw two people dance so perfectly and so gracefully together. He was also taken back by the beauty of Elfriede and her lovely Arctic blue eyes. His mom Ingeborg, noticed the look and stare on His's face.

She grabbed his arm, nudged him and said, "Ask her to dance, I'm sure she will be delighted."

"No, I'm not that good of a dancer," he said, his eyes locked on the circling, graceful, pirouetting. "Look at them, Mom. They are beautiful together, just beautiful! Have you ever seen a father and daughter dance like this before? It's magical."

His mom reached over and grabbed a single rose. She handed it over to her son and said, "A beautiful lady will never turn down a gentleman that offers a rose."

Her son looked at the rose and paused for a moment, he swallowed and felt a lump in his throat the thought of dancing was intoxicating, but he had not danced in years. He then made his way over to the center of the courtyard near the fountain. There he waited holding on to the rose and watched as Elfriede and her dad danced toward his direction. As they got closer, Elfriede noticed the young man standing next to the fountain with one hand behind his back. Then with no hesitation, the young man made himself noticed and caught the eye of Elfriede as she and her father brought their dance to a halt. He held out his arm and offered her the rose. He then bowed and asked, "Would you care to dance?"

Elfriede was taken back but gracefully accepted the invitation. A warm feeling that made her blush somewhat was also noticeable on the young man's face. They continued to dance and to his surprise he matched her step by step as if they'd danced many times before. The young man and Elfriede danced together for a while sharing stories. That's when Elfriede flashed back to her childhood, and recognized the young man. "Eugene?" She said.

Her calling him by name caught him off-guard, so much so that he tripped over Elfriede's feet and landed face first on the ground. "Elfriede?" He said, pulling himself back up onto his feet.

The two of them chuckled for the longest time. Elfriede told him what had happened and why her father and herself stopped coming to the weekly festivals. Elfriede was on top of the world, never in a million years did she expect to rekindle with her childhood friend.

The afternoon festivities began to wind down and Elfriede said goodbye to her old friend.

Eugene gave Elfriede a warm hug, said goodbye to her and Gustav and returned to his mother. Elfriede then excitedly ran up to her father and shouted, "This was the happiest day of my life, Father!"

He said, "I know, darling, it was a wonderful birthday indeed." Gustav was a gentle, loving man but couldn't fight the urge to feel a little jealous over the attention Elfriede had shown to Eugene all afternoon.

Adalwolf and the Shadows

Many miles from the beauty of the lush Black Forest and Elfriede's village was a land that most have forgotten. A kingdom not many would dare to visit, and rumored not to exist at all. Here was the kingdom of King Adalwolf and his Queen, Marianne. Perched high on the cliff of a steep, stark mountain stood their black limestone castle. Covered in crystals of snow and ice, the castle of Adalwolf and his Queen shimmered like sugar on black licorice. Adalwolf was a strong and powerful king with dark hair and sharp sideburns. He dressed in black, carried a sword and wore a long cape lined in ruby red silk. He routinely practiced his skills in the dark arts, he worked hard honing them routinely, on a daily basis. He strived to be the most powerful sorcerer in the realm, he embellished on the fact that his name struck fear into his enemies' hearts. Each morning and evening Adalwolf would conjure his army of shadows and spar with them. His shadows came from a place of darkness, they were from the world beneath the realm of they lived in. Immortal minions that could only be controlled by the darkest of sorcery.

His Queen, Marianne, was like no other queen, she was beautiful like most queens but the raven black hair that flowed behind her, was long enough to touch the marble floors she walked on. She was a queen who had everything a queen could ask for... but still she was sad and never satisfied. The opulent castle had its grand ballrooms and endless vestibules decorated in stained glass. Hung from above were the magnificent chandeliers that would glow and sparkle during the evening. This was the perfect place for countless hours of entertainment and dance. When darkness fell and the candles were lit, Adalwolf and his queen would dance these empty halls and ballrooms till the early hours of morning. The three step waltz and the traditional laendler were a few of the favorites the two of them would share together throughout the night. But this evening, something was wrong, something was missing as Adalwolf stared into Marianne's eyes. He could see the unhappiness and unrest in her heart.

"What's wrong, my dear?" asked Adalwolf.

Marianne said, "I feel empty, there was a time when I could feel the music and myself as one. It would carry me into the most magical places that I could dream of. But now it's gone, missing from my heart."

Adalwolf was taken back and never wanted to see his lovely queen disappointed. He was a strong man and a powerful king and always found a way to give his queen everything she wanted. Now this was something he had a tough time trying to solve and fix. The next evening, he retired to his stateroom where he would practice sorcery and plan his next conquest. Like so many nights before, he began his ritual of chants and dark practices. Mysterious smoke filled the room as he cried out and flashes of orange and purple shook the castle walls. Then with an almighty crescendo, he would summon up his army of minions. Swirling high above and swooping down from the heavens arrived the Shadows. The Shadows were fiercely protective and loyal to their master. Along with Adalwolf, they were responsible for his success and reign over the surrounding villages. Adalwolf pleaded with the Shadows for help with his situation of Marianne's unhappiness. Adalwolf called upon his minions to fetch his rare ingredients for a glimpsing spell, "I need a Pegasus feather, tears of a mermaid, the scale of a dragon, and hydra venom. Go quickly my minions and do not fail me!"

After impatiently waiting for several hours his Shadows poured back into the castle and swirled amongst the tapestries that hung above, Adalwolf channeled his energy into his Shadows and conjured up an image out of crimson fire and smoke. Suddenly, Adalwolf heard this beautiful music followed by the image of Elfriede dancing so happily with her father in the town square. The magic and beauty between both of them was like nothing he had ever witnessed. The Shadows began to show him the music box that was given to Elfriede.

In a raspy hiss they said, "The music box is very powerful and bestows the gift of music, dance and true love and is blessed by all good things that matter the most to its rightful owner."

With that said, Adalwolf knew with utmost certainty he had to get his hands on this music box. He fell into a meditative trance, pitch-black smoke flowed from his hands encasing his lanky frame. The Shadows began swirling in a fevered pitch that was clearly orchestrated by Adalwolf as he carried out his sorcery and battle cry. "To the forest!" he shouted. "To the Black Forest we must go!"

Along with the wind howling, you could hear thunderous chants cascading from the castle of Adalwolf and Marianne. Flash! Crackle! Boom! Fire and crimson smoke billowed throughout the castle. Alarmed but highly excited, Marianne ran into the room where she saw this spectacular vision of choreographed madness. She glanced over at Adalwolf and saw that familiar look on his face, determined, ruthless and out to conquer anything he chose. This was the man, husband and king that Marianne loved the most.

"Come with me," he said, "together we will find that magic and happiness you so desire and long for."

With a devilish look and half of a smile, Marianne locked arms with Adalwolf and looked up at the castle ceiling. Circling in a frenzy the Shadows swooped down, engulfed the two of them and swirled back up into the chaotic maelstrom they had created. With one last sonic boom and a flash, the purple and orange storm shook the castle walls and made its way out of the kingdom and off into the night. It was only a matter of time before Adalwolf and his horrifying Army of Shadows would arrive in Elfriede's village in search of the magical music box.

Shall we dance

It was a busy afternoon and a long day back in the village. Elfriede and her dad were finishing up for the day packing up their cart. Elfriede was blooming with excitement as she stared across the courtyard smiling at Eugene. Both of them were distracted throughout the day paying no attention to their work. When everything was put away and her tasks were completed, Elfriede ran over to see Eugene. "Shall we dance?" she asked.

"Why yes I would like that," Eugene said. Again with her music box close to her and the lid open, both of them danced off into a musical bliss.

Shortly thereafter, Gustav while looking on decided he wanted to share a dance with his daughter. So he walked over and politely asked, "May I have this next dance?"

"Yes you may!" Eugene exclaimed.

Off went Elfriede and her dad sharing a few steps that only the two of them knew how to perform. Looking over was Eugene's mom, she was ready to go home for the day and growing impatient. As the minutes passed, Eugene knew if he was going to spend any more time with Elfriede that afternoon, then he would have to cut in and take Elfriede's hand once again.

So he swooped over as Gustav was ready to swing Elfriede around in one of what was many graceful circles. "May I cut in please?"

"Yes," grumbled Gustav. It was the polite thing to do even though he was still enjoying the wonderful dance he shared with his daughter.

Gustav with his head down, decided to walk away toward the edge of the courtyard. He then continued to tie down what was remaining on his bread cart. Gustav watched his daughter dance with the young man. He always feared that this day might come that his daughter would fall in love and later move on with her life, leaving him behind, all alone. Elfriede was his most precious possession, without her life seemed almost meaningless. He stood there watching them a few more moments before calling out to his daughter. "We must head back before we lose too much sunlight."

Elfriede said goodbye to Eugene before skipping over to her father and then they made their way back home. Gustav was happy for his daughter's newfound friend, but felt empty as fear of losing all those special moments they both shared gripped him like the jaws of a wolf.

A day to remember

The next morning Elfriede sprung up from bed after a long night's sleep. She opened her window and glanced outside. As she took a deep breath the aroma of tiger lilies and dahlias enraptured her and reminded her of Eugene. It was another joyous day and Elfriede was more excited than ever to get to the village. Her mind was whirling as she danced and sang to herself while preparing breakfast for her father. Gustav would use this time to finish baking his last batch of rolls before sitting down to eat. Sitting across the table Gustav noticed that Elfriede barely touched her breakfast and now was up hurrying toward her bedroom.

"You haven't touched your breakfast!" Gustav exclaimed.

"I'm not hungry," she said. "I need to get dressed and fix my hair."

Gustav rolled his eyes and grinned; he could now see clearly that his daughter was in love. He also knew that someday he would have to let her go. As sad as that seemed, it was meant to be. Shortly after breakfast Gustav was outside loading up his cart with his baked goods. He then shouted to Elfriede, "Are you almost done?"

"Just a few more minutes!" she yelled back. Elfriede couldn't decide what dress to wear and fiddled with her long, silky, blonde hair till it was just right. Then as her father yelled for her one last time she called, "I'm coming, I'll be right there!"

Without missing a step, she began to sing and dance as she made her way outside to join her father. As they made their way off the beaten path through the thick, dense forest and halfway to the village Elfriede realized she'd left her music box at home. She asked her father if she could go back home to pick it up.

Gustav said, "No, darling, we are running late and we must continue to the village."

She was remembering how special her music box was and how it had brought her and Eugene together. Without her music box things might not be the same. Elfriede then once again pleaded with her father, "My music box means the world to me and I must go back and get it."

Reluctantly Gustav said, "Ok, dear but please hurry, I will continue to the village without you and get everything set up before the first customers arrive."

Elfriede hugged her father and said, "Thank you, I promise I will be back shortly!" With a quick turn and a hop in her step, she began her journey back to the cottage.

It was a pristine day in the village as Gustav arrived and began setting up his cart. The sky was bright blue with puffy little white balls of cotton like clouds rolling along. The birds played in the water under the center courtyard fountain as the townsfolk arrived, serenading them with happy chirps.

Pretty soon the village square was filling up and the street vendors were busy at work, like a well-functioning hive of bees. Gustav was selling his bread and muffins at a brisk pace. He looked up to take the next customer's order and found himself looking straight into the eyes of Eugene. "Good morning young man, how are you today?"

Eugene studied Gustav hovering near him. "I'm fine. I was surprised and a little concerned when I saw you working alone, is Elfriede okay?"

Gustav ran his fingers through his salt and pepper hair. "She forgot her music box and should be back shortly. But If you could check on her for me, I'd appreciate it."

"Very well," said Eugene, "I will head back toward your cottage and meet up with her."

"Thank you," said Gustav, "and yes, please find her and come back swiftly."

Ok, sir, I will!"

Eugene then ran back over to his mother and got permission to leave. "Goodbye, Mom, I will be back shortly."

Eugene made haste into the forest. He noticed that the sky began to grow dark and ominous. The sun became shrouded and started to fade away slowly. In the distance a thunderous groan promised bad weather. It grew louder by the minute. Gustav looked up and exclaimed, "A thunderstorm? This early in the day? That doesn't seem right."

This also caught the attention of everyone else in town as the villagers scrambled to brace themselves for the incoming rain. These particular clouds didn't behave like normal rain clouds, they swirled in one direction and then changed course abruptly.

Gustav thought this was strange and then began to make out images of terrifying creatures emerging from the darkness. Their glowing eyes were in perfect focus now.

"The Shadows!" cried Gustav. "The Shadows! Run everyone!"

Panic then struck the village as everyone braced themselves for the arrival of Adalwolf and his army. Adalwolf and his army of Shadows were a local legend and not believed by some, especially this far away deep in the Black Forest. But the folklore was turning into reality right in front of their eyes. Adalwolf and his queen Marianne soon arrived riding on the backs of the last group of Shadows that descended into the courtyard. The air was difficult to breathe for the villagers and their eyes burned from all the caustic smoke. With a slash from his sword, Adalwolf cut through one of the many traditional flags that flanked the town square.

Rising up imperiously he announced, "I am here in search of a magical music box! Bring it to me and I will bring you no harm!"

Gustav was trembling with fear knowing his daughter owned this mysterious music box. All he could think of was her safety and what was going to happen next. The villagers knew nothing of this music box that Adalwolf spoke of, but Gustav did.

As tension started to build and time ticked away Adalwolf became impatient. Not one villager stepped forward to hand over the music box that he had demanded. And without further hesitation he unleashed his army of Shadows to destroy the village.

Buildings were set ablaze and soon began to tumble down to the ground forming scorching hot piles of ash. The flames spread over the town out of control and smoke billowed into the sky filling the air with its acrid smell, and the pathetic cries of the helpless town folk. Gustav decided to make a last-ditch attempt to run from it all and head into the forest to find his daughter. He was just leaving one of the last buildings still standing when he saw a blinding flash, and then came a final blow from the Shadows as the roof above crashed down on him before he could escape.

Panic in the village

As Eugene met up with Elfriede, they could hear the sound of horror on the wind and desperate cries for help off in the distance. Both scared, they knew something was very wrong. Eugene then grabbed Elfriede's hand and said, "I must go back and help. I need you to stay, it will be safe here in the canopy of the forest, I'll come back for you!"

Elfriede agreed and watched as Eugene dashed off to the village without her. Standing there alone in the forest she held on to her music box tightly for comfort. She nervously glanced around the wood at every little sound, expecting the worse.

As Eugene arrived in the village he was slack-jawed, overcome with shock and astonishment. Most of the village was destroyed and only a few homes remained. He heard a familiar voice call, "Eugene!" It was his mother, covered in black ash but still alive.

"Mom!" he cried out. They hugged each other for a long moment and then they began to walk around looking for friends and any other survivors.

***

Back in the dark forest, alone, scared and confused, Elfriede felt hopeless. She worried desperately about her father and if he was ok. He was her world and she couldn't bear to wait any longer for Eugene to return. Without hesitation she knelt down and placed her music box under a large fern that grew under a tree. She would come back for it later knowing she would travel faster without it. She then began to climb over a rock pile which led to a shortcut through a woody bog. This would be the quickest way back into town unnoticed.

Once she arrived back into town, the sight left her wide-eyed with grief. She let out a short sob of horror but immediately silenced herself. She hurried, picking her way through the rubble and broken glass looking for her father and Eugene.

She then came across a few villagers and in a trembling voice she asked them, "Have you seen my father?" All she got was blank stares.

***

Eugene had been wandering around, stunned and confused. At that moment he heard a familiar voice, turned around and saw Elfriede standing there alone, her face a mask of horror. He yelled over to her, "I told you to wait for me back in the forest!"

She ran over to Eugene and flew into his arms and said, "Have you seen my father?"

"No," he said, "most of the village is destroyed but I can hear plenty of cries for help, I'm sure we will find him."

They searched their way and followed the cries for help lifting up the debris and pulling out survivors. Then as they came across a pile of twisted wood, Elfriede recognized a familiar pair of shoes. "Father, Father!" she yelled.

Eugene began to remove the pile of broken glass and twisted wood only to find the lifeless body of Gustav. Elfriede gasped for air and shrieked, "Father!" She then collapsed on her knees and cried what seemed like a lifetime resting her head on her father's chest.

Elfriede's heart was broken, she trembled and saw her life pass before her eyes.

Eugene wrapped his arm around Elfriede and held onto her tightly. "There is nothing we could have done, we could have been killed ourselves if we stayed here in the village."

***

A moment later marching only feet away was Adalwolf; he looked pleased and satisfied by the carnage he caused but was still frustrated not finding the music box. But then as he was ready to gather up his army of Shadows, he glanced over and saw Eugene and Elfriede. "I know that girl," he said, "I remember her face! She was part of the visions that brought me here to find the music box. She was dancing together with an old man... Now I remember, she is the one I'm looking for!"

Adalwolf then charged in their direction, sword in hand. Alerted, Eugene spun around to see Adalwolf charging toward them. Frightened, he jumped up, noticed a plank of wood that was laying on the ground and picked it up. He then positioned himself standing protectively over Elfriede. Within seconds the two weapons met with a loud thud. Slash... crack.... and metal to wood echoed through the air. The two of them battled putting on quite the show.

The Shadows then swarmed in, searched through the rubble and circled around Elfriede. They were frantically looking for the music box but found nothing.

Adalwolf, his face twisted and contorted in rage searched Eugene's eyes and yelled, "Where is the music box? I'm done toying with you!"

Eugene knew to keep his mouth closed, to say anything would only cause more harm for Elfriede. Demonstrating remarkable prowess as one of the top swordsmen of his village, he proved too be a formidable foe, even with a wooden plank, and continued to battle toe to toe with Adalwolf. Then out of nowhere Adalwolf stopped dead swing and grabbed the wooden plank from Eugene with is free hand. "I told you I am done toying with you, if I wanted you dead you would be already. I've decided you are more valuable to me alive, at least for now," Adalwolf said, and then chuckled to himself.

Adalwolf called upon his army of Shadows. He yelled to them, "Take him alive! I have other plans for him."

Overtaken by the Shadows, Eugene's weapon was knocked out of his hands. The Shadows swarmed and engulfed him only to whisk him away up into the smoke-filled sky. Adalwolf now with his with his queen alongside, followed close behind and shouted, "Back to the kingdom!"

Marianne questioned Adalwolf about the music box. Adalwolf only replied, "I will hold him as a prisoner and with that, the music box will find its way to me...you shall see!"

***

Elfriede still kneeling on the ground was shaken. She was now all alone, the entire village was slaughtered, besides the few that managed to flee like Eugene's mother and it was now growing dark. Tears streamed down her face as she looked down at her father's lifeless corpse and said one final goodbye. Her dad who she loved so much was gone along with Eugene and the village she called home. Not knowing what else to do, she picked herself up and ran back into the forest. She dashed through the woody bog and over the pile of rocks without hesitation. As she headed down the path that would lead her home, she suddenly realized that it wouldn't be safe to go there. The only other direction she knew of was to travel through the Fern Blackwood's. This was a section of the forest that only Elfriede and her father would explore together. It was the most beautiful part but very dangerous. Her father would speak of mysterious creatures and dense fog that could prevent any visitor from returning. Like a carpet, the majestic ferns and countless flowers littered the forest floor. And from high above, only streams of light would cascade down through the tree canopy like golden fingers. It was a magical place indeed, but shrouded in mystery.

Scared but determined, Elfriede continued to run and make her way into the woods. She wanted to get as far away as possible from the place she used to call home. Dashing through the ferns and jumping over the flowered shrubbery, Elfriede raced into the unknown. Eventually she came across a small clearing in the forest. A bubbling brook ran through the glen. Exhausted and out of breath, she dropped to the ground and leaned up against a large rock. This could be a safe place to rest, she thought. The gurgling sound of the brook helped her relax, she was both mentally and physically exhausted. No sooner then she set her head down, Elfriede fell asleep.

Elfriede meets Teodora

For a couple of hours, Elfriede quietly rested under the canopy of trees undisturbed. The sound of music danced in her head as she began to wake up after a well-needed nap. A warm loving essence vibrated through her body. She wondered, am I still dreaming? It was a good feeling, the same feeling she'd had the first time she danced with Eugene in the town courtyard. But something was different, it was stronger than she ever remembered and the reason she was awakened. As her vision improved and she wiped her eyes, she noticed her music box sitting in front of her. Startled, she jumped up and took a few steps back. "How is this possible?" She thought. Her thoughts rambled. Who, what and why? Feeling a little hesitant, she bent down to pick up her music box. It was a sight for sore eyes and this clearly made Elfriede smile, but she wondered how it arrived. She only remembered leaving it hidden under a tree before she ran back into the village. Suddenly she heard a rustle, crunch, and a crack! "Who's there?" she snapped.

Elfriede turned around, looked off into the forest only to notice some branches and a few ferns wafting in the breeze. The sounds were getting closer as Elfriede continued to stare out into the dense foliage of the forest. She then noticed what looked like two eyes pleasantly looking at her through the green tapestry that was slowly moving toward her.

"Don't be afraid, darling," a voice whispered softly. And with that said, a small creature emerged and came into view. The creature held out its hands and spoke again. "Yes, don't be afraid, my troubled one. I am Teodora."

Elfriede was taken back at first but somehow she trusted this little creature. Cautiously, she accepted Teodora's hand and tilted her head in curiosity. Teodora was much shorter than Elfriede but very beautiful. She had long golden hair that sparkled and draped below her shoulders. Her entire body glittered and was covered in ferns and leafs from the forest. Still hesitant and a little afraid, Elfriede said, "Hello, my name is..."

Teadora interrupted and said, "Yes, I know who you are, welcome to the Fern Blackwood's, my love."

Surprised and still holding the music box with her other hand, she began to feel it vibrate again and emit a wondrous glow. Teodora said, "Your love and compassion for those around you is very strong, dear... this is what the music box tells me.... and this is how I found you."

Elfriede started to smile as she tightened her hand around Teodora's but then grew sad thinking of those she had lost recently. Seeing her sadness, Teodora reached up, grabbed the music box and placed it onto the ground. Then in a playful manner, she sprung up and began to spin around gracefully with both arms out creating the most beautiful lines any dancer could have. As she came to a close, Teodora then gestured toward Elfriede to join her. Instinctively, Elfriede followed her lead, jumped and spun into a fouette as did Teodora ending in an elegant fourth position. Teodora looked over and smiled; she then proceeded with a few more steps that led into a grand jete before pausing again. Elfriede would then go on to copy the same dance moves just as Teodora performed without missing a step. Together the two of them danced and laughed as they whisked themselves around the forest floor.

Feeling revived and in a happier state of mind, Elfriede became more comfortable with Teodora. The two of them made their way over to a large log. They sat down on the log next to each other and giggled for a moment. Elfriede said, "That was wonderful! I had so much fun."

"You're welcome, dear, you're such a beautiful dancer," said Teodora, "the most talented dancer I have ever seen."

"Oh...thank you," Elfriede said, "and thank you for returning my music box!"

"You're welcome, dear, it was your music box that found you."

"Found me?" asked Elfriede.

Teodora placed her hand on the music box, looked up at Elfriede and said, "Your music box is very special, it's filled with magic and all good things. It has connected with you."

Her new friend's words were rather confusing. "Connected with me?"

"Yes...and this is how I found you. Only a special person can connect with the music box, someone who is pure and truly loves...someone who feels the magic of music and dance. You are this special person, Elfriede. The magic it holds can be very powerful and used only for good things.... acts of kindness, joy and helping others."

"Oh my," said Elfriede. "I don't know what to say...my music box... magical... powerful."

Teodora said, "Yes...some things you will find here deep in the Fern Blackwood's are indeed mysterious and magical. This is why so many fear to travel into these parts of the forest. But I need to warn you, dear, this beautiful and powerful gift of yours will always be at risk."

"At risk? Why?" asked a now even more confused Elfriede.

"There are others who seek the music box... others who practice sorcery and dark magic. These individuals will stop at nothing to harness the powers of your music box and use them for personal gain and destruction. This is why we must go...we must leave. Always in danger you will be without protection."

"Well, I have nowhere to go," said Elfriede. "I am all alone, I lost everything that was dear to me and have no family."

Elfriede broke into a sob, resting her face on her hands. Teodora was a nice momentary distraction, but now the reality of her being alone loomed heavy over her head, like a storm cloud threatening rain. Tears pooled in the corner of her eyes and streamed down her cheeks.

Teodora took Elfriede's hand. "Hush child, you're in the Fern Blackwood, the most magical place in this realm. If there is any place in the world that can cure sorrow it is here." She said, reaching into her belt pouch.

Teodora revealed a small glass vial with pink fluid inside, fitted with a cork on top. She popped the cork and offered it to Elfriede. "Think of your worst memories and then drink this potion dear. It will help you forget your troubles temporarily. You need a clear mind for the task at hand, if you want to save your friend."

"Eugene...flashing back to him vanishing into black smoke and being whisked away, leaving her alone and feeling helpless to save him." Elfriede gasped. She then titled the potion to her mouth and thought of all her worse memories and swallowed it down.

At first she felt no different, then a warm and fuzzy sensation enveloped her and all of the horrible memories of her past, such as her mother dying of fever and her holding onto her father's lifeless corpse, now felt so distant that she was numb to them bad feelings.

Teodora was well aware of the recent events that haunted Elfriede and could now see the sadness fade away from her as the potion took hold. She also knew that something had to be done to rid the land of Adalwolf and his dark magic. It would only be a short time before he would invade the Fern Blackwood's in search of the music box and cause harm to all the creatures that lived there. As Elfriede continued to grow sad, Teodora knew exactly what she needed to do to ...something magical.... something wonderful that would imbue Elfriede with strength and confidence.

Teodora cracked a small grin as she turned and looked out into the forest. She nodded her head gently and waved her arms somewhat into the air for a moment. And just like that the forest started to come alive. From behind the rocks and ferns beneath the trees, emerged a group of creatures that appeared out of nowhere and slowly gathered around the two of them. These were beautiful creatures Elfriede thought, and they looked a lot like Teodora but much taller. Some of them had long wings that draped down to the ground and others did not. Then she faintly began to hear this wondrous symphony that filled the air. It was a familiar sound that was warm and loving. She then realized it was a melody of music that all the creatures were singing together in unison. How wonderful she thought, it sounded something like crickets late at night in the forest as they all chirped together in unison. Still a little startled but excited, Elfriede let out a deep breath as two of the creatures approached her. Each of the creatures reached out and grabbed one of Elfriede's hands. They then led her away from Teodora over to a large clearing on the forest floor. That familiar vibration of warmth and love started growing stronger. The creatures were now circling her.

Elfriede stared in wonder. "Oh my, what is this?".

Her body began to tingle and sparks of beautiful light danced all around her. The intensity and brightness of the swirling sparks began to crackle and pop louder and louder. A little scared, Elfriede decided to close her eyes for a moment. Then just like that the maelstrom of crackles and pops went silent. There was a cry of happiness and joy amongst Teodora and the creatures as they let out a cheer. This piqued Elfriede's attention again so she quickly opened her eyes. She looked out at everyone and saw the biggest smiles and happiest faces staring directly back at her. Then all together Teodora and the creatures gracefully took a bow toward Elfriede as if she were a queen. Astounded by all the attention and feeling loved, Elfriede smiled and curtsied back to her audience. She then noticed while looking down at herself that she was magically adorned in a glittery white dress. "Oh my!" she cried, "how beautiful!"

Her new dress shimmered and sparkled slightly just like Teodora and all the others. An elegant tiara that shimmered brightly and reflected into the forest now perched regally atop her head. "How magical!" she exclaimed. "How magical indeed. Thank you! Thank you!"

The Journey

Elfriede was smiling again and feeling the love from her new group of friends. She felt beautiful and confident like Teodora had hoped that she would.

"It is time to leave, off we must go," Teodora said.

"Go where?" Elfriede asked.

"We must travel east to the Gardens of Belvedere, there we will find an old friend of mine, he can help us!"

"Who?"

"That's not important, dear, we are running out of time...we must leave now!"

Elfriede was slightly perplexed, but trusted the words of Teodora. She grabbed her music box and held it tightly. "Yes!" she spoke up, "let's go then!"

Teodora summoned a handful of her winged creatures to join them on the long journey. Almost instantly they swarmed over to both of them and crouched down low to the ground. Teodora was first, she happily jumped up onto the back of one of the creatures. Elfriede cautiously walked over to the other winged creature, climbed on and nervously said, "Ok, here we go!" And with that said, swoosh! Off they went darting up through the tree canopy. Elfriede's heart filled with excitement as they climbed ever so swiftly toward the treetops. She had never flown before and found it absolutely exhilarating, she took notice to how differently things looked as they gained altitude. She looked down one last time to wave goodbye to the remaining creatures of the Fern Blackwood's, thinking to herself how tiny they all looked.

Their glow and magical sparkle began to fade away slowly as they flew upward toward the darkened sky. The entire group traveled through the night with the help and navigation of the stars above. Elfriede marveled at the beauty of traveling like this, it was fast but peaceful and felt a lot safer than she'd ever imagined.

The night soon became morning and the first glimpse of the land below came into view. Teodora in a commanding voice spoke, "Welcome to Austria!"

Rubbing her eyes to get a better look, Elfriede could only say, "Spectacular!" As far as the eye could see, rose the majestic snow covered Alps of Austria. In the valley nestled between the mountains were tiny villages surrounded by green grass and fields of wild flowers. This was a land Elfriede had only heard stories about and saw mention of in books but had never seen with her own eyes.

"Wow, it's breathtaking! Are we there yet?" she asked.

"Almost," Teodora replied, "but now we must rest and continue by foot."

"Continue by foot? Why?" asked Elfriede.

"The Gardens of Belvedere are sacred and must be approached slowly," said Teodora.

As the group touched down, Teodora instructed the creatures to stay behind and rest in the fields outside the village. She also had them look after and guard the music box as it would be noticed if brought into the nearby village. As Elfriede and Teodora made their way toward town, Teodora spoke up and said, "I know the perfect place to relax and have a good meal. Follow me."

The quaint village of Salzberg was a lot like Elfriede's, the town was beautiful and the residents seemed friendly. There was music everywhere and the smell of hot oils and fresh baked goods filled the air. Elfriede then noticed that some of the town folks were starting to stare at the two of them. Teodora right away exclaimed, "We need to blend in with the rest! I need to dull down my magic and find you a traditional dirndl made here in the village."

Elfriede loved her sparkly new dress but understood the need to change into something more practical. Without using her magic and bringing attention to themselves, Teodora grabbed Elfriede's hand and walked over to the nearest dressmaker's shop. Once inside, Teodora instructed Elfriede to pick out something without delay.

"Here, this one will do," said Elfriede as she made her way to the dressing room toward the back of the shop. A few minutes later she came out wearing the new dirndl and holding onto her sparkly dress. She then headed over to the counter where the dressmaker was standing. The older woman looked up at Elfriede and said, "Why the rush honey? Are you sure that's the dress you want?"

"Yes," Elfriede said.

The dressmaker then said, "I can see that you're from out of town. Kind of strange to be traveling in such a beautiful dress?"

"Yes, we are just visiting but won't be here for long, we are on our way...."

Teodora hushed, then cut off Elfriede and said, "Come, dear, we must go."

They both thanked the dressmaker after purchasing the dress and made their way toward the door. The dressmaker scratched her head with curiosity and watched the two of them leave the shop. Then for a moment her eyes lit up as she concluded her suspicion. She ran to the back of the shop and out into the alley where only the shop owners would gather and softly cried out, "Messenger! Messenger! She's here!"

She repeated herself once more and with that, a shadowed figure emerged creeping its way toward the dressmaker. "Yes, what is it?"

"She's here! Let Adalwolf and the Queen know that she is here and on her way!"

The shadowed figure then asked, "Does she have the music box?"

The dressmaker said, "I did not see it, but I'm sure she still has it. I sensed the magic between both of them and knew they were hiding something...she was also traveling with one of those creatures from the Fern Blackwood. Pease give Adalwolf and the Queen this message!"

This shadowy creature was indeed one of Adalwolf's Shadows. A messenger left behind for one purpose, and that purpose was to alert Adalwolf and his queen to the location of the music box and its owner. Satisfied with this new information, Adalwolf's Shadow twisted its image from humanoid to that of thick black smoke and speed up into the sky above leaving a fading squid ink trail behind. The dressmaker engulfed with smoke and ash stood there as she watched the Shadow return to Adalwolf's castle.

The Message is received

Adalwolf's castle soon came into view as the Shadow began its approach. It circled the kingdom a few times and flew low to the ground kicking up powdery snow in its wake. Swoosh! Roar! There was a howling sound from outside that rang throughout the castle and alerted Adalwolf. Feeling excited, he jumped to his feet and ran up to the stateroom where he practiced his sorcery. With haste he quickly opened up one of the stained glass windows. Moments later the Shadow spiraled downward and entered the castle through the open window. Adalwolf waved his hand up in the air and summoned the Shadow to come before him. And with that command, the Shadow finally came to rest, manifesting into a solid form before Adalwolf. "What is it?" he the king demanded. "What do you have for me? I must know!"

The Shadow spoke of the dressmaker and how she encountered two outsiders from another land that seemed to be in a hurry. Adalwolf listened closely and replied to the Shadow, Hmmm, did they have the music box?"

The Shadow spoke again, saying, "No... but there was this young girl and she was traveling with one of those creatures from the Fern Blackwood."

"Yes! That's them! A creature from the Fern Blackwood's would never leave its home unless they are in danger!" He then continued, "Yes, my plan has worked! They come for the boy and hope to have him rescued!" Adalwolf then gave out his order, "Send out a group to head them off before they reach the castle...immediately!"

***

Shortly after Elfriede and Teodora marched out of the shop, Elfriede looked down and spoke of her new dress. "I actually love it, it's very much my taste for something I picked out so quickly that is."

The two of them giggled for a moment, then Teodora spoke up. "Here it is!"

About three shops down from the dressmaker was the delightful eatery of which Teodora had spoken. "Let's go in, you will love the delicious food that they serve."

Once inside, they walked toward the back of the room where a large stone fireplace was roaring. "Here, this table will do just fine," said Teodora. They sat down and got comfortable next to the fireplace and perused the menu. Misty eyed and a little tired from the journey, Elfriede found herself glancing into the fireplace. Something was a little odd about the flames that caught her attention. She rubbed her eyes and squinted a little to get a better look. Hmmm she thought, what is that?

Swirling inside the fireplace were ghostly images that seemed to be formed by the fire and smoke. Shadowy figures that somewhat looked familiar. Interesting she thought, they reminded her of the creatures that swarmed and destroyed her village. Teodora noticed Elfriede's attention to the fireplace and asked, "You see things don't you?"

"Yes I do!"

"What are they?" Elfriede whispered.

"The connection with you is strong," Teodora said. "Even though you are away from your music box, it has the power to show you visions and future events."

Elfriede then interrupted and said, "I saw those evil Shadows. And what looked like a great snowstorm and soldiers in battle!"

Teodora paused biting her lip and then said, "Interesting, they must be aware that we are coming. We must eat quickly and continue on to the gardens of Belvedere."

After finishing their meals, they paid for their food and exited the shop. Soon they passed through the center of town, Elfriede observed the same activity from the residents and street vendors that were present in her village. There was someone that sold bread, and others that sold fruit, vegetables and flowers. Flowers! she thought. The aroma of flowers filled the air, and this reminded her of Eugene. "Eugene!" she said out loud as she paused looking out into the courtyard. "I hope he is ok."

This was the first time Elfriede really thought about anything bothersome since leaving the Fern Blackwood's and was surprised by how numb she was to the thought of Eugene. The potion did not make her forget, as she remembered every detail of all the bad memories that she shielded herself from. It just felt like they happened a lifetime ago, or in another life.

Teodora continued to march on as if she'd heard nothing. There was a concerned look on Elfriede's face and a faint sense of urgency. But she quickly snapped out of it and walked at a brisk pace to catch up with Teodora.

The Gardens of Belvedere

As the afternoon grew old, Elfriede and Teodora soon arrived back to the outskirts of town. They stopped at the edge of the field where they'd arrived earlier and the creatures were still there waiting on them. Once more Teodora waved her hand slightly and called out the winged creatures. Like the day before back in the forest, one by one they magically appeared coming into view. Elfriede was amazed how the creatures could blend in with the natural surroundings and remain hidden. Teodora spoke to Elfriede earlier during the trip and explained how this was a survival skill that all the creatures used to camouflage themselves for protection and safety. Teodora then entered the field and circled the creatures and spoke up. "Alright everyone! Let's go! And this time we walk!"

So the group gathered together and marched onward as Teodora instructed. One of the winged creatures that was protecting the music box walked alongside Elfriede and placed it back in her hands. "Here you go, dear," the creature said.

Elfriede rubbed her fingers gently over the polished surface of her music box pleased to have it back in her possession and replied, "Thank you! Thank you for looking after this! What is your name, sweet one?"

The creature smiled. "My name is Karlotta."

"Karlotta." She said turning the word into two syllables. Elfriede smiled at her. "That is a lovely name, nice to meet you," she said in a bubbly voice.

Karlotta then commented, "I can see your music box brings you so much happiness, you clearly are connected and very fond of it."

"Yes indeed, it was a gift from my father. I will cherish it for the rest of my life."

The two of them talked together over the next hour or so as they giggled from time to time sharing childhood stories. Elfriede was starting to feel like her old self again. She was always good at making new friends and took a special liking to her new friend Karlotta. Karlotta was a little more talkative than the other creatures, who mostly only talked amongst themselves. The group eventually stumbled upon a narrow pathway as they headed deep into the valley. The pathway looked hardly used and was thick with overgrowth.

Teodora remarked, "This is the best way to reach the Gardens of Belvedere without being noticed. It is a very sacred place, so we must proceed quietly and with respect."

Elfriede was taken back a little after hearing Teodora's remarks. Sacred place? Approach quietly? she thought...hmmm. "I thought we were going to meet an old friend," she mumbled to herself.

It was a long day for Elfriede, Teodora and the creatures. The sun was setting and things began to grow dark as the group eventually made their way out of the forest. Now with the overgrowth and narrow pathway behind them, Teodora stopped. She gazed down into the valley below and quietly announced, "The Gardens of Belvedrere."

And with that said, Elfriede whispered, "Oh my, it's beautiful." Gazing off into the distance and down into the valley, Elfriede took in what looked like a majestic palace illuminated by the bright moon high above, the moonlight reflected off the white stone monolith, making it visible for miles. The palace was surrounded by an enormous garden filled with decorative fountains and neatly trimmed hedges and trees. Elfriede was amazed at how these elaborate gardens were laid out in such detail, almost like a maze. Again Teodora announced, "Let's continue, everyone...we don't have much time."

So the group slowly walked down the hill and began to approach the palace arriving at the front entrance. All that stood in front of them now was a grand wrought iron gate with a height of about 12 feet. It was locked but Teodora quickly waved her hand and clankety-click, the lock sprung open and the gates grinded open at a snail's pace. The group made their way in and walked down one of the many pathways that were lined in tall neatly trimmed shrubbery. The night air was becoming cool and a haunting mist started to blanket the grounds. Elfriede mumbled to herself, "If we are here to meet someone, why must we visit at night when it's cold, dark and quiet?"

Teodora heard Elfriede's soft remarks and quickly replied, "You will understand soon enough my dear."

The group made one last turn and walked out of the maze of shrubs and into a large open area inside a courtyard. There stood a majestic fountain in the center with cascading waterfalls that filled three huge, marble pools. Neatly lined up and down the courtyard were countless rows of stone and bronze statues. Elfriede walked over to one of the many statues and quietly asked, "Soldiers? Horses? Who are they?"

Without answering her question, Teodora interrupted Elfriede and spoke up in bravado, "Here you are. General Kristof! It's so good to see you my old friend."

Elfriede was puzzled and a little confused, why was Teodora speaking to a statue?

"Come here, dear, I want you to meet someone. This is General Robert Kristof."

"What?" Elfriede said. "What do you mean? He's just a statue."

Teodora said, "Yes indeed, but he was the greatest warrior the Austrian army has ever had! He died long ago and is considered a national treasure to the people of Austria. The Gardens of Belvedere have been the home for General Kristof and his army for many years. It's a sacred place, a memorial celebrating the countless battles he fought to protect and save his people."

Elfriede was surprised and still a little confused but interested at the same time. She looked up at the statue and marveled at its beauty. The General was a handsome man and looked very accomplished as he valiantly sat up on his horse wielding a fearsome sword. He was clearly a decorated soldier with countless medals adorning his uniform. Frozen in time, it was a striking monument that displayed the General in all his glory. How wonderful and noble was Teodora's story.

Elfriede then asked, "How is this General Kristof going to help us? This is just a statue. I thought we came here to seek his help?"

Teodora quickly answered her. "Yes we did, and he will help us. Be patient my dear, he will help us."

The Awakening of General Kristof

Elfriede slowly walked away from Teodora and strolled down to view some of the other statues of General Kristof's men. The moon above was bright and lit up the statues throughout the garden. Elfriede became fixed on the soldiers' appearances and how true to life they seemed, she inspected them thoroughly. The detail of each sculpture was astonishing, she had never seen artistic sculpting such as this. It seemed almost magical. The soldiers looked strong and confident as some had a look of victory plastered in their eyes and others bolstered a bravado while sweat ran down their faces. Breathtaking and surreal, Elfriede continued to study the men and seemed to be captivated in the moment. Visions started to appear to her of each soldier and his past...they looked so vivid that Elfriede could even hear the men shout as they fought alongside each other in past battles. Then the visions slowly faded and faintly off in the distance, Elfriede could hear something unusual. Bong! Bong! she heard this every four or five seconds. What is this? she wondered. A church bell? Yes, it must be a church bell ringing slowly off in the night she concluded. This snapped Elfriede out of the trance she was in and brought her back to the present. She thought this was strange, and wondered why a church bell would ring this late at night? With every strike the bell pealed a little louder sending goosebumps racing up and down her arms.

Then suddenly, that familiar chorus of voices and electricity started to fill the night air. Elfriede looked over at Teodora and the creatures and noticed that they were conversing with themselves quietly in a mysterious language. The group gathered into a circle surrounding the statue of General Kristof. Elfriede craned her neck, watching with curiosity and could only stare as she watched this strange but familiar ritual. The chants and the clanging of the church bell became louder and louder by the second. Dashes of light and pretty sparkles swirled around the group and then became fixed on the General and his horse. Then out of nowhere, Elfriede felt a tear run down her cheek and onto her lips. She was overwhelmed with feelings of love, empathy and a sense of gratitude. It was her music box again, connecting her with the others and bringing on this flood of emotions once more. It was also clear that these feelings of love and gratitude were shared by the entire group and solely directed toward the Statue of General Kristof. As she continued to look on, the General and his horse began to glow with a multitude of vibrant colors.

Crackle...bang!...crackle!...sparks exploded into one last crescendo and boom! After a few moments the air that was consumed with smoke began to clear and the moonlight returned to grace the courtyard. Still standing in front of the group, Teodora took a few steps forward. She cracked a smile and spoke up in her stern loving voice. "General! Welcome back!" An eerie silence that followed.

Elfriede took a deep breath, then swallowed hard and spoke to herself slowly...all she could manage to squeak out was, "Oh my!"

The statute of General Kristof, now magically stood before her alive and in the flesh. Elfriede could not believe her eyes. The great General Kristof was awakened after all these years. He sat regally atop his horse in all his glory and full of life. Slowly the General dismounted and walked over toward the group. He then stopped and bowed gracefully, the way only a highly distinguished military man could, in front of Teodora and the creatures. With a slight grin and a bit of bravado he said to Teodora, "It's a pleasure to see you again, my lady."

Prisoner Eugene

The hours seemed to tick off slowly and time stood still. Confused and alone, Eugene remained a prisoner in one of the many chambers of Adalwolf's castle. Surprisingly, he was in good shape and was left unharmed after his confrontation with Adalwolf and the Shadows. As he paced back and forth inside his chamber he wondered, why me? And why do they want that music box? He could only imagine what had happened to his mom, Elfriede and the surviving villagers after he was whisked away. This worried him immensely and made him feel helpless. Eugene knew if he had any chance of escaping and returning to the ones that he loved, he would need to remain calm. With those thoughts, he slowly began to feel a new sense of calm and determination. Outside his chamber, there were two Shadows standing guard that prevented Eugene from escaping. He could only wonder the evil origin of these black entities and what dark sorcery conjured them up. The stories about them were very true, they were indeed horrific and haunting just as he had been told. They were something not from this world, he was sure as he looked on and continued to study them. They mysteriously hovered off the ground and were comprised of a thick black smoke that took on the shape of their ever changing bodies. And if you were to get close enough, you could even smell the sulfuric odor of burning brimstone that lingered in the air all around them.

As a young boy the stories of Adalwolf and his Shadows were spoken about often. These were stories told by the elders as a harsh reminder not to travel outside the safety of the village. Most villagers considered these stories as just folklore, but now unfortunately Eugene knew these stories to be horribly true. Then he heard footsteps off in the distance, becoming even more noticeable as the seconds ticked on. Eugene wasn't surprised by the ever changing creeks and scuffs that echoed throughout the castle's halls and corridors. This was caused by the endless corridors and secret rooms and magnificent marble floors. It was hard not to notice the beauty of Adalwolf's castle. Strangely, it seemed too beautiful to be a place where such evil and harm could be conjured up. Then a familiar voice addressed Eugene as the owner of those footsteps finally arrived and entered his room.

"What do you know about this girl? What plans does she have with this music box?" Adalwolf demanded to know.

Startled at first, Eugene paused for a moment and shrugged. "I know nothing that you ask. Please let me go!" he demanded.

Adalwolf shook his head, laughed and walked closer to Eugene. He stared straight into his eyes and grinned. "I will learn soon enough! Your girl and her friends are walking right into my trap! They are no match for me and my army of Shadows!"

Eugene pulled against his restraints until the blood drained from his hands and then issued a stern warning, "If you harm my Elfriede even one bit…I will find a way to escape and destroy you here myself!"

With that last remark, Adalwolf smiled and laughed some more as he abruptly turned away and made his way out of the chamber. Again his footsteps echoed throughout the castle, but this time they slowly faded away into the distance. Eugene felt a lump in his throat after this last remark towards Adalwolf. But he meant every word he said. He then wiped the nervous sweat from his forehead and walked over to one of the windows. Looking out he saw mountains of snow and the vast empty wasteland that surrounded the castle. It looked frigid and bleak, with no signs of life. This again began to worry the young man as his thoughts focused back on Elfriede and the mysterious friends with whom she was traveling. Overwhelmed with emotions of sadness and fear, Eugene turned away from the window.

Stay positive he told himself, everything will be alright. He glanced over at the two menacing shadows and then took a deep breath. "I can do this. I will find a way!"

United

The creatures could only smile, as well as Teodora and a startled Elfriede. General Kristof politely greeted the group of new friends and began to pace back and forth slowly. As he did this, he studied his subjects from top to bottom and displayed a friendly grin. Teodora then spoke up. "General, we need your help!"

Kristof focused his attention on Teodora. "What is it, my lady? What's troubling you?"

"These are difficult times," she said. "Our world and way of life are in danger. The evil Adalwolf and his Queen Marianne are growing more powerful and threaten the lives of everyone across these great lands. Through his dark sorcery, Adalwolf has learned the origin of our sacred magic and the individual that holds its key. My dear friend Elfriede is this special person. She's the one, the one who is pure with love and kindness. Together with her music box, Elfriede is at risk of being captured. Adalwolf will find a way with his dark sorcery to unlock the powers of the music box and destroy all that is good with Elfriede. We must protect Elfriede and prevent Adalwolf from getting his hands on the music box."

The General paused a moment after hearing Teodora's plea. His facial expression grew very concerned as he looked over at Elfriede. He clearly could see that he was no warrior and need his aide. "This is troubling indeed," he murmured to himself. A sense of urgency was apparent, as was the familiar smell of war. The General turned around and stared off into the courtyard and its expansive gardens. Row after row, the men of his great army stood proud amongst the surrounding shrubs and trees. Suddenly the visions of past conflicts and battles flashed through his head, followed by the triumphant roars of victory. As these thoughts continued to play out in his head, Kristof experienced a sense of comfort and camaraderie. The General knew of nothing else, but to fight...fight for what was good in the world. "Well. What are we waiting for!" he shouted. "I need my men!"

Teodora's face lit up with excitement as she spoke up and said, "Yes! Let's awaken the soldiers!"

A sigh of relief and a new sense of hope ran through Elfriede's head. More than ever, she felt loved and gained some well needed confidence to continue on.

Teodora wasted no time and gave out her instructions. She told the creatures to spread out into the gardens alongside the many soldiers cast in stone. And just like before, that familiar ritual of chants soon followed. Electricity and sparks filled the air giving Elfriede goosebumps once more. Colorful streams of light danced above her head creating a loud buzz much louder than before. Crackle! Swish! Pop! The Gardens of Belvedere were now alive and breathing, the countryside surrounding them glowed with surreal light that could be seen from miles away. Pop! Bam! Crack! Soldier after soldier sprang to life before Elfriede's eyes. It was truly magical and one by one, General Kristof's grand army of soldiers were united once again.

From ear to ear, Kristof displayed a cunning smile. His men, his soldiers, his family were back again. He wasted no time in giving out his orders. Like clockwork, the soldiers took formation and with one crisp gesture saluted their commander in chief. It was remarkable, powerful and beautiful all at the same time Elfriede thought. She felt overwhelmed with emotion and ran up to the General. Kristof broke his composure as Elfriede embraced him with a warm hug. She then looked up at him and said, "Thank you! Thank you, General. I lost everything dear to me and now all I have is you and my new friends." She then finished off by saying, "Can you help me?"

Kristof then regained his composure and like a father, using a stern voice he said, "My dear, everything will be alright. Don't worry." Kristof paused a moment then turned back around and looked at his army.

"Prepare and brace yourselves, men! We have a battle in front of us like we never faced before!""

There was no denying what was at stake. They would soon engage in a war with an enemy that used the ways of dark magic and sorcery. But Kristof was proud and very confident in his men. He knew in his heart that good always triumphs over evil and his men would taste victory once more. He served as commander in chief for many years, and never lost a battle.

Dinner for Two

Adalwolf and his queen were settled in for the evening. It was dinner, and the table of offerings was plentiful. The chandeliers were lit and glowing softly. Like most nights, Adalwolf and his queen sat at each end of the grand dining room table. Each of them would speak sparsely but gazed into each other's eyes as they enjoyed the elaborate spread of food. The relationship between Adalwolf and his queen was very passionate. As evil and cruel as they were, they loved one another dearly. Maybe this was because they both shared the lust for power, riches and all things that served them. But something was different about this evening, something Adalwolf sensed shortly after sitting down for dinner. His Queen Marianne was extremely quiet, she spoke very little. She was distant and looked lost. Adalwolf grew concerned and as dinner ended, he walked slowly over to his queen. As he approached her, he held out his hand and asked Marianne to dance. She abruptly declined his offer. Adalwolf felt defeated and softly said, "What's wrong, my love?"

With tears filling her eyes, Marianne spoke up and said, "My passion and love for you escapes me. I now feel empty and need something more. How can I dance when I feel nothing?"

"But my love," Adalwolf said, "give me a little more time...I will give you all that is lost and much much more."

Marianne shook her head and turned away, she then got up from the table and slowly walked away. This saddened Adalwolf once again, but soon his sadness turned into rage. Like the flick of a switch, Adalwolf reached for his sword and began destroying everything on the dining room table before him. The food, plates, candles and glass shattered into a million pieces. He then let out a horrific roar and dashed up the grand staircase and up to his room. He fell into a meditative trance and then started chanting in an unknown tongue, he conjured up his dark sorcery and the castle walls began to shake. Adalwolf had to glimpse his future, as his wife was everything to him and he was not ready to lose her love. He raised his hands above his head chanting even louder and then swirls of flame and flashes of sparks consumed his room, and mysterious images began to appear on the canvas of smoke that was created. These visions soon became a little clearer, it was an army he saw, a grand army engaged in battle. The look and feel of this vision seemed very familiar, it was a place Adalwolf knew all too well. It was the snow covered valley that led up to his castle. This concerned Adalwolf, but he understood what he was seeing in this vision of the near future. "The girl and her friends, now have a grand army," he whispered to himself, then his voice suddenly grew louder. "If it's a battle they want! I'll show them a battle they'll never forget!"

Spinning around and looking up to the castle ceiling, Adalwolf then began to conjure up more shadows, thick black smoke enveloped his entire being, his chants echoed through the castle as he called into existence ancient shadow warriors, larger than any he had ever conjured before. He sent them off to join the others the new shadows towered over the others, they were over double their size. "Their grand army will be no match for my army of darkness! They are clearly walking into my trap just as I planned." The walls continued to shake violently as Adalwolf's sorcery came to a climax.

This abruptly awakened Eugene who was imprisoned on the other side of the castle. It was the first time he was able to sleep since his arrival. He jumped up out of his bed and focused his eyes on the doorway where the shadows once guarded. They were gone now and Eugene thought, wow! How can this be? Something wasn't right after seeing the absence of the two trusted guards who watched over him.

Still off in the distance, he could hear the thunderous commotion within the deepest parts of the castle. Then suddenly, the noise and vibrations stopped. Eugene paused and took a deep breath. He then found himself reflecting upon his thoughts and past troubles. "Click… click…click." Eugene jumped! Startled and confused, Eugene felt his heart stop. He yelled out, "Who's there?" Who is it!? Three more times he heard those few clicks again, but this time they were a little louder. The sound was coming from the window. Slowly he approached the window as he tiptoed through the darkened room. As he reached the window, he peered out while wiping the frosted glass to get a better look. "Hello," a voice whispered.

"Hello, you must be Eugene."

"What! Who are you?" he then said. As the moonlight permitted, Eugene started to get his first glimpse of the mysterious person who spoke to him. Hovering in the air behind the glass was a creature. A beautiful creature with two long wings and a peaceful smile. The creature then spoke again. "She's coming. She's on her way! Elfriede's coming," she repeated.

"Elfriede? How do you know Elfriede? And who are you?" Eugene asked.

"I'm Karlotta, my dear, Elfriede is on her way and she will be here soon."

Eugene was baffled. "Coming here? Elfriede?"

"Yes, she is with General Kristof and his army."

"Army, what army?"

Karlotta then interrupted, saying, "We must go, there will be a great battle. You won't be safe here, even behind these castle walls!"

After hearing all of this, Eugene's eyes lit up. He grabbed a chair that was close to him and swung it into the window smashing the glass. Karlotta wasn't surprised and made her way through the opening and into Eugene's chamber. Eugene paused a moment after his actions and then pushed away the broken glass beneath him. He was confused but somewhat excited at the same time. As strange as it sounded, he believed this strange creature. "OK...tell me what I must do?"

Karlotta examined Eugene's shackles and waved her hand using her magic to release him from his restrains. The cold iron shackles clanged against the stone floor. Then she held out her hand and spoke. "Quickly, we must go, climb up on my back!"

Eugene rubbed his wrist they were sore from the shackles. "Thanks for freeing me Karlotta."

"No time to get emotional, we have to get going before anyone notices us escaping."

Eugene grabbed Karlotta's hand and just like that, found himself atop of her back sitting securely between her wings. They made their way through the opening of the window and swiftly flew away from Adalwolf's castle. Eugene felt the bitter cold wind sweep across his face. He then looked down upon the frozen wasteland and grinded his teeth at the frigid temperatures. Fading away in the distance, he looked back once more at Adalwolf's castle. Those images of Adalwolf and his terrifying shadows would soon be far behind him and just a bad memory.

Swish! Off into the moonlit sky, Karlotta and Eugene dashed out of sight.

The Silver Storm

As General Kristof gave his final instructions to his men, Teodora rounded up her creatures. Elfriede, not knowing what to do next, found herself pacing back and forth wondering what was to come. As she mingled amongst the creatures, she found herself seeking the whereabouts of her new friend Karlotta.

She called out, "Karlotta. Karlotta!" She was nowhere to be found.

Teodora looked over and saw a concerned Elfriede. She then asked, "What is it, my dear?"

Elfriede said, "Oh nothing. Everything's fine."

Teodora looked puzzled, she then turned around slowly and went back to her duties. Elfriede watched Teodora walk away. She shrugged and spoke quietly to herself. "Where is she? She must be around here somewhere. Oh well, I'm sure I'll find her soon."

Teodora and General Kristoff were now standing together. They were front and center of both the creatures and the soldiers. The General then spoke to Teodora with his authoritative but respectful voice. "So, my lady, where does this battle take us this time?"

Teodora quickly replied, "We must cross the valley and pass over the snow-covered Alps. Adalwolf's kingdom lies on the other side."

Kristof then barked out his orders. "Ok, men! Line up! Formation! March!"

With that order hundreds of clanking shields and armor came to life, and the large body of men rhythmically fell into order, like a swarm of worker ants ready to please. With a clear direction in hand and a mission to be accomplished, General Kristof and his men headed out of the courtyard and into the valley. Teodora, Elfriede and her creatures gathered together soon after and followed close behind. Like before, the safest way to travel was under the cloak of darkness, and with the illumination of the moon above, the beauty of the distant Alps remained spectacular. Now that the group was larger with the addition of Kristof and his army, more than ever did Elfriede feel safe and a new sense of comfort. She was still haunted by the past events of tragedy but with the help of the potion she felt mostly numb to those events, but she still wanted justice. But now she focused her thoughts on Eugene. Where exactly did Adalwolf take him? And was he still alive? Elfriede pondered every possibility, and then decided he was probably alive and being used to bait her. Then suddenly from behind, Teodora reached out, grabbed her hand and spoke. "My dear, don't worry. We will do everything in our power to help you, and to find your friend Eugene." Like before, Teodora always knew what was troubling her friend.

Elfriede instantly felt a sense of relief and smiled briefly. As she looked back at Teodora, she saw nothing but goodness and kindness from a band of creatures from the Fern Blackwood's. It was puzzling why there were legends of not traveling into these parts of the forest. They were indeed mysterious creatures, but far from dangerous as she had been told. But some legends are told for the purpose of protection, and reasons not to disturb. Elfriede now knew this to be true.

Eventually the group found themselves at the base of the mountain range. The first signs of sugary snow now appeared in front of them. It was draped over the wooded pines and blanketed the forest floor. More than ever, the reflection of the moon from the snow lit up the forest. It was awesome, Elfriede thought. How could a countryside so close to the kingdom of Adalwolf and all his evil, be so beautiful?

As the hours passed, the group ascended up to the top and slowly back down the majestic mountain that once confronted them. Now laid out in front of them, was one last valley neatly tucked between the surrounding Alps.

It was much colder now, ice and snow clung to everything in sight. There was still no view of Adalwolf's kingdom even though the night passed and morning arrived. It was a beautiful morning as the sun and its warmth touched Elfriede's skin. The look of relief and smiles appeared on some of Kristof's men. But this moment of warmth and additional light suddenly shifted. As quickly as the sun and all its glory appeared, dark ominous clouds filled the sky. Out of the east, a frigid cold air swirled all around them. Now the skin on Elfriede's face started to tingle as panic spread amongst them like wildfire and concerned talks could be heard amongst the crowd. The ice and snow beneath everyone's feet began to rise slowly off the valley floor. Everyone looked at one another in disbelief. Teodora clearly looked concerned; she immediately spoke up and said, "He knows we're here. Adalwolf knows that we're here!"

The sky above began to grow darker and the snow continued to rise up to the heavens. General Kristof couldn't believe what he was seeing. Yes, it was snowing, but it was snowing in reverse, this wasn't normal. Those dark clouds above also looked strange…very strange. He began to say, "Those aren't clouds!"

But Teodora cut him off and shouted, "The shadows! Brace yourselves! Take cover!"

Clearly now, the blackness that hung above them began to take shape and descend speedily as the snow funneled back up into the sky. This created a maelstrom of confusion and havoc, it was something General Kristof and his soldiers had never seen.

"Well then…we fight!" he shouted to his men. Kristof said a battle chant that made the swords of his army glow with bright white light, they looked divine and his men held their swords skyward and screamed a battle cry in unison, "Deus vult" and charged into battle with the attacking swarm of shadows. The flood of blackness continued to pour down from the sky above.

Teodora then directed her creatures to intervene and disrupt the flight of the shadows as best they could. She knew all about Adalwolf and his shadows. She also knew it would be very difficult to fight them off, even with help of Kristof's army. She shouted to the group, "The only way to fight off this sorcery is to defeat the sorcerer himself! Forge ahead, everyone! We must continue toward Adalwolf's castle!"

The swarm of blackness from the shadows mixed with the whiteness of swirling snow created a silver looking storm that now blanketed the valley.

Crack! Swoosh! Sizzle! The battle raged on as the shadows became tangled along with Teodora's creatures. Elfriede could not believe her eyes, those peaceful creatures she knew only hours before, fought fiercely alongside Kristof's soldiers. It was impressive and a sight she would never forget. The humming sound they made evolved into an earsplitting roar and grew louder by the minute. Kristof and his men were clearly having a difficult time engaged in battle while being blinded by the silver storm created by Adalwolf's sorcery.

A dozen of the giant shadows now appeared on the battlefield, in front of the General and his group of men. His men ran in front of him by the dozens forming a shield wall to keep their leader safe.

General Kristoff studied the situation and then shouted, "Archers ready your bows." He then paused awaiting the giant shadows to get closer. "Loose!" He commanded.

Hundreds of arrows rained down on the giant shadows, they swatted at them furiously and confused, as if a swarm of wasps were swarming them. The General then had his men lock in the creatures with their shields, making a wall around them. The shadows were strong and sent many of good men flying shields and all, but each time more men moved in and took their positions.

Teodora fell into chant blessing the General's sword. After the enchantment ended, Kristoff raised his sword to the heavens and bolts of lightning called down from the sky striking the giant shadows with precision. "Finish them." The General ordered.

His men went from barricading the giants to now bashing and slashing at them for all they were worth until they were destroyed. As each shadow fell to their blows they would explode into heaping piles of gray ash.

As this frightening scene continued, Elfriede suddenly found herself separated from the group. She was now breathing heavily and found herself taking shelter under a tree. Still clutching tightly to her music box, she glanced off into the distance and caught a glance of Adalwolf's castle. Shivering from cold and fear, she rested a moment. Worried about her safety, she then made the decision to run off toward the edge of the forest into the thick pines. Immediately as she entered the forest, she was confronted by a small group of shadows that took notice and swooped down blocking her path. "Oh no!" she screamed. Her face grew pale and her body began to tremble in fear.

"She still has the box!" cried out one of the shadows. "Grab her!"

Elfriede saw the group of shadows slowly moving toward her and let out another scream for help. They were almost upon her when something strange happened, the music box began to glow, Elfriede could feel its warmth flowing throughout her body, but this time it was much more intense than before. She felt herself become lighter as a soothing melody poured from the box and she floated off of the ground a few feet. Her eyes began to glow bright white and then a surge of light exploded out of her chest making the nearby shadows flee. The light beamed skyward from Elfriede like a beacon of light, from a lighthouse and pierced the endless cloud of shadows above. Thunderous sounds could be heard as the cloud swirled and changed forms, before fading into nothingness and revealing a blue sky above. The remaining shadows fled the battlefield retreating back to Adalwolf's castle as they realized what conspired, only a handful of shadows remained on the battlefield engaged in combat.

The light dimmed down and the melody slowed to a stop. Elfriede felt drained, she never felt so weak in all of her life. Before she could process what just happened she collapsed to the ground.

***

From the air Eugene scanned the land below for any sign of Elfriede, he had no idea what was going on but the intense light he saw moments earlier left him on edge. The battlefield was busy with moving bodies which he found very distracting. Eugene was determined to find Elfriede and keep her safe.

Eugene almost lost his balance as Karlotta went into a freefall unannounced.

"What are you doing?" Eugene said. "You nearly tossed me off your back."

"I see her... oh dear."

Eugene spotted her as well laying sprawled out on the snow covered ground unconscious. As they neared he noticed a small group of shadows a few yards out approaching her. "Drop me off over there," Eugene demanded.

Karlotta circled the shadows, Eugene didn't wait for her to land, he launched himself off of her back and pummeled the shadows, taking them by surprise.

She then flew over to Elfriede and landed just behind her motionless body.

Elfriede felt a swoosh of cold air from behind her and heard a loud thump hitting the ground a moment earlier. A stern but familiar voice called out to her, "Are you OK dear?" Karlotta said. "Grab my hand, we must go it's not safe here."

Elfriede struggled to reach her hand out to the familiar voice of her friend Karlotta. With some effort Karlotta managed to get Elfriede onto her back.

Karlotta looked back at her, examining how the music box had weakened her friend. "You have a very deep connection with your music box," she said. Then she flexed her back to roll Elfriede onto her stomach. "You may not have noticed but you've turned the tide of this battle, your music box and yourself somehow disrupted Adalwolf's cursed storm of endless shadows, the remaining shadows have fled or been vanquished."

Elfriede dug deep to pull out a few more words, as she felt almost lifeless. "No idea how I done that, I was scared and then it's like the music box came alive, like it has a mind of its own," she took another breath. "It saved me, like it put a protective barrier between me and the shadows."

Moments later Elfriede caught a glimpse of someone that was now confronting the shadows a few yards off.

"Yes!" Elfriede replied faintly. "But who is...who is that?"

Karlotta smiled.

"It's Eugene!" she shouted.

That loud thump Elfriede previously heard must have been Eugene jumping off the back of her friend, right before Karlotta rescued her. Eugene was now engaged with the shadows wielding a sword that he'd just picked up from the battlefield. Elfriede couldn't believe her eyes, it was Eugene, and he was alive just yards away from her. Swoosh! Slash! Eugene quickly discovered that if you slash your sword enough times through the smoked-filled body of a shadow, it would disrupt their sorcery and scatter them into ashes. Eugene was determined this time not to be defeated. He fought swiftly and efficiently, and with a dozen or more slashes of the sword, the final shadow was turned to ash. Eugene let out a breath of relief and paused for a moment. He then ratcheted his eyes firmly on Elfriede and dashed over to her. Elfriede began to weep softly, laying weakly on top of her friends back. He wrapped his arms around Elfriede and held her ever so tightly. Elfriede sniffled away her tears briefly and spoke, "Are you alright? I missed you so. I missed you so much!" She then looked up at Karlotta and could only say, "Thank you...you found him."

Karlotta smiled and said, "I knew how important he was to you, dear, and everyone else if we are to stop Adalwolf and his destruction. I went ahead without the permission from Teodora and broke the rules. She doesn't always agree with me and my crazy ideas, but this time I think she would concur."

Eugene then interrupted, declaring, "We must go! The battle has now moved toward the castle! Karlotta, take us to the castle quickly!"

"No!" Karlotta protested. "It's not safe!"

"Don't worry, I have an idea, fly us low under the trees so we are not detected, and head over to the north side!"

"You better be right," Karlotta flapped her wings. "Off we go to da castle."

Battle of Swords

Queen Marianne stood staring out the window of the tallest turret of Adalwolf's castle. She watched as the approaching army made its way up to the castle grounds without any resistance. Suddenly behind her Adalwolf appeared and spoke up. "I guess I must take this matter into my own hands!" He hissed.

"Don't worry, my love, I promised you that music box, and I intend to deliver with on my word!"

Marianne glared back at her king with a selfish scowl and said nothing, she had no words of encouragement for her husband. She then turned slowly and continued to look out the window. Adalwolf's desperation now grew into sheer anger, he stormed out of the room and down the endless spiraled stairwell. This was a battle he was determined to win, at all costs, he thought. This battle was no longer for himself, but for his kingdom, and most importantly, his wife.

***

Eugene, Karlotta and Elfriede arrived un-noticed at the north end of the castle. Eugene's plan was to do a flanking maneuver, by sneaking back into the castle while the battle raged on the opposite side. Now armed with a sword and feeling more confident, Eugene wanted to take Adalwolf by surprise. As he knew this would be his only chance of gaining the upper hand. Karlotta learned of this new idea and cried back to Eugene, "I told you the battle here at the castle will be very dangerous. We must leave and keep Elfriede and her music box safe from Adalwolf and his sorcery!"

"Then you go!" Eugene shouted. "Take her back deep into the valley behind the approaching battle, she will be safe there. I need to finish what Adalwolf started, and rid these lands from his reign of terror! I must face Adalwolf again for as long as blood runs through his black heart, Elfriede will remain in danger!"

Eugene then leaned over and gave Elfriede a kiss which brought some blood back into her cheeks, making her blush. He hugged her tightly once more and shouted, "Now go! I will come back for you when it is safe!"

Elfriede cried back, "No! You must stay with us! I'm not losing you again!"

Eugene said nothing and felt conflicted with emotions. Grinding his teeth with determination he walked away from Elfriede. There in front of him was a servant's door that was unguarded and led into the castle. He opened the door gently trying his best to keep it from creaking, he glanced around inside for a moment before he entered.

Before Elfriede could relish his presence Eugene was gone again. She wept as the potion did not numb her to these new feelings and she fell to the ground. Karlotta knelt down beside her and spoke. "My dear, don't worry...his love for you is very strong. I feel very confident that you will see him again. He will return to you. Now we must go. Climb onto my back and hold tight."

Elfriede picked herself up and wiped away the tears that were running down her face. She was starting to feel like herself again, she was still a little drained, but more like over worked and ready for bed, compared to having no energy at all. She then climbed up onto Karlotta's back, secured herself and her music box. Then they swiftly soared into the air toward the valley. As General Kristof and his grand army reached the front gate of the castle, the remaining shadows swarmed them like angry wasps. Still they fought strong and valiantly, there were only a few wounded and no fatalities. Teodora had her hands full orchestrating her creatures and distracting those pesky shadows. Her magic could only be used for good. Conjuring up a magical spell for inflicting pain onto others was not something any creature from the Fern Blackwood's was permitted to do. So she would conjure up large thorn bushes to protect her companions and allies, and use her powers to mend minor wounds the injured. One by one, Kristof and his soldiers also learned the sword technique that turned the shadows into ash. Explosions of this splintered ash fell from above as the shadows swooped down upon the group. The smell of this was overwhelming as flashes of fire and brimstone left the men's faces black with soot.

The group finally reached the castle and proceeded to fight off the remaining shadows. Kristof thought for a moment that his group could be heading into a trap as they made their way inside.

Adalwolf now reached the bottom of the stairs arriving in the grand foyer of his castle and found himself confronting his enemy. He looked around quickly and noticed the carnage and weakness of his army of shadows. Most of them were defeated and turned to ash. This enraged him! He let out a fierce roar, stomped his foot firmly to the ground and held out his sword. He then cried out, "General Kristof! You were the talk of legend and presumed long dead…I'm not sure what magic brought you back to face me again but this time I will see to it, that you will never walk these lands again!"

Then a voice cried out from behind Adalwolf, "Not if I have something to say about it!" It was Eugene. He sprung out from the darkness slashing his sword downward and nearly striking Adalwolf as he was caught off guard. Seconds later, the two of them were locking swords and in full battle. Metal to metal, clash!…cling!…clang! Both opponents struck swiftly calculating each other's moves perfectly.

General Kristof and his men were only yards away from this dueling sword fight. Kristof looked concerned and knew this young man was no match for the powerful skills of Adalwolf.

Just as the General was ready to run over and intervene, Adalwolf raised his free hand, said a chant and sent Eugene's sword flying through the air like a projectile, it slammed into the castle wall with great force leaving it stuck in the rock.

Adalwolf looked satisfied with his move. "I told you before boy, I have no time for these childish games with you."

With another wave of his hand Adalwolf took the breath from Eugene's lungs, black smoke formed around his feet and poured down his throat, he dropped to the ground defenseless and gasping for air. Just then, two shadows jolted over and grabbed ahold of Eugene and held him captive.

Adalwolf looked at his minions sternly. "Take the boy back to his prison, I'll deal with him later."

With lightning precision, Kristof jumped and spun through the air slicing through the four remaining shadows that stood between him and Adalwolf, the shadows fled behind this master. After completing this remarkable move, Kristof landed only a few yards away from the glaring Adalwolf. The two of them paused a moment, glowering ferociously into each other's eyes. The castle then grew silent. All the creatures, soldiers and remaining shadows fixed their eyes on the anticipated duel between Adalwolf and Kristof. Both opponents were fixated on each other, blocking out any outside distractions. Even Adalwolf didn't notice the sudden entrance of his Queen, Marianne, who quietly made her way down the stairwell and perched herself one floor above the grand foyer overlooking the activity below.

Flanked on each side of the queen were two giant menacing shadows which she kept near for protection. As she looked down, she could see both men slowly circling each other, anticipating one another's moves like a game of chess. They were intensely focused and never losing eye contact. Adalwolf snarled and spoke again. "I'm quite impressed, Kristof, your army is strong, very strong...Yes, it's the music box and its magic that brought you here. Teodora was wise to awaken you...but now she and her creatures will suffer the consequences for bringing you here and challenging me! Soon, I will defeat you and your grand army, and the music box will be mine!"

Kristof took a few steps toward Adalwolf and with a calm and assuring voice said, "It is you that will be defeated, Adalwolf, surrender now and maybe I will let you and your queen live."

Adalwolf glanced down at his sword and paused a moment. His anger and frustration rose to a new level. He sneered his contempt. He then pumped out his chest and growled, "Never!" Before General Kristof could blink an eye, a lightning fast strike from Adalwolf nearly took him down. Kristof was lucky to respond in time and block the oncoming blade. Crack! The powerful clash of swords stunned the crowd of onlookers as both men sprang into action. Clang!...Crack!...Bang!... the sharp metallic crash of both blades connecting sent shockwaves throughout the castle. Both men exchanged spectacular moves at a blistering pace. There was energy in the air, electricity danced the length of the Generals blade as it crackled in a wave of energy around it. Shadows swirled like small tornados the length of Adalwolf's blade, each strike was truly a duel of light versus darkness.

Eugene felt his heart pumping as he could only look on as a spectator, the smoke that suffocated him was now gone and he could breathe normally again. He wanted so much to join in and fight alongside Kristof, but was unable to free himself from his captors.

Teodora also looked on and grew concerned. She knew there was nothing she could do, these two powerful men had to settle this war between themselves. This was a duel to the death that was grand and epic in scale. Clearly, one man would be defeated and the fate of the people and the surrounding lands hung in the balance.

Clang!...Crack!...Each man displayed expert swordsmanship as they continued to battle. Only a few minutes passed by, but it seemed like forever.

Perched up on the balcony above, Marianne's face was wreathed in concern. Her husband, the great warrior that he was, usually struck down and defeated his enemy within seconds. Adalwolf's confrontations were usually swift and victorious. Nobody had ever held out and survived as General Kristof. Was the great stone warrior now weakening? He seemed to stagger. Though her husband's opponent was impressive, and his name legendary, but he appeared to be losing ground.

***

Back in the valley waiting safely, Elfriede and Karlotta took shelter. Elfriede soon began to grow impatient as terrible thoughts raced through her head. She then spoke up and said, "Please, Karlotta, we must go back! I need to be with Eugene and the others."

Karlotta replied, "My dear, it is not safe. Eugene made it clear, he wanted you and your music box as far away from Adalwolf and his castle as possible."

"I know, Karlotta, but Eugene is all I have. I can't lose him again! Please!"

Elfriede pleaded with Karlotta over the next hour as she paced back and forth with nervous energy. Against Eugene's instructions, Karlotta finally gave in to Elfriede's pleas and said, "Ok dear, I will take you, but if we find ourselves in the littlest of trouble, I'm bringing you back!"

Elfriede's eyes lit up and her heart raced with excitement. Again, holding tightly to her music box, Elfriede positioned herself on Karlotta's back. Karlotta's wings began to flap furiously, blowing the fresh snow off the ground below, a few steps and a jump, and they launched into the air. Elfriede surveyed the valley below, it was now peaceful and not a soul to be found. The pristine white snow that blanketed the ground, was now littered with black ashes, the waste and the burial ground for the defeated shadows. This gave the valley a strange greyish hue which was haunting and unpleasant to the Elfriede's eyes, something she would never forget. Karlotta then spoke up. "Are you sure you want to go back?"

"Yes," Elfriede said resolutely. "Yes, I'm sure!"

Then off in the distance, Adalwolf's castle came into view. As small as it looked from a distance, it still looked menacing. Elfriede's stomach started to rebel in fear, but there was no chance she was going to stop, even though the fear made her heart race. All she could do was close her eyes and think of good things that brought her some relief. This time, Elfriede was determined to make a difference. She would need to be strong, and find a way to help Eugene and her friends.

As they landed, the battle raged on between Adalwolf and Kristof.

Clang!...Crack!...Swish! Both men were trading blows at a fevered pitch displaying super velocity and speed. The onlookers remained quiet, wide eyes frozen in their expressions as they continued to watch this epic duel. The sound from the swords clashing together grew even louder and was deafening at times. Teodora and a few of the creatures found themselves covering their ears. Still watching, Eugene's heart raced even as beads of sweat collected on his face. He tried with all his strength to break free from the shadows that held him tight.

Then from across the room echoed a familiar voice. "Eugene!" Startled for a moment, Eugene searched for its source. It was Elfriede, she was climbing off the back of Karlotta. She ran over to the balcony railing that was opposite of Eugene, Marianne and her shadows.

Eugene called out, "Elfriede!"

The commotion now caught the attention of Marianne. Her eyes lit up with surprise and excitement as she saw Elfriede. There she was, that mysterious girl and her sought after music box. Marianne knew all too well how important it was to capture this young girl and exploit the powers of her music box. The secretive powers of the box could only be unlocked by its chosen one. But the chosen one could not be harmed, it was critical that both the girl and her music box remain safe as they were tethered together as one. "I want the girl! And I want that music box!" Marianne shouted.

She then spotted a group of shadows that were perched together on a catwalk across the foyer. She pointed the shadows in the direction of Elfriede and demanded her capture. Swiftly awakened from their idled stance watching the fight below, the group of shadows jousted toward Elfriede and Karlotta. This small group of shadows swarmed over both of them, one by one trying to grab a hold on Elfriede. Outnumbered, Karlotta did everything she could to fight off and protect Elfriede. This enraged the shadows even more as they increased their attack. Elfriede now found herself separated from Karlotta and pinned up against the balcony railing. She was frightened more than ever as she continued to cling on to her music box. She began to scream, as fear took over her emotions.

Hearing her cries of terror, Eugene mustered up the strength to finally break free from his captors. He shouted, "Elfriede! Be strong! I'm coming to get you!" And with that said, Eugene looked up and saw the grand chandelier suspended from above. He dashed over and jumped up onto the railing. Then he took a deep breath making a leap of faith and successfully grabbed hold of the chandelier, which now swung violently as Eugene positioned himself on top holding on to the chain.

He then continued to shift his weight from side to side to increase its momentum. Holding on tightly, he then approached Elfriede's balcony moving closer with each swing.

Elfriede then cried once again, "Help! Eugene, help me!"

Eugene shouted back, "Jump! Come to me! You can do it!"

Elfriede looked up and saw Eugene swinging from the chandelier and cried, "Are you crazy! You want me to jump? "

"Yes! You can do it!"

Elfriede then swung her arm one last time fighting off one of the shadows but dropping her music box. There was no time to turn around and pick it up, she climbed on top of the railing and looked for Eugene. Then without hesitation she closed her eyes and jumped toward the chandelier as it swung its way back. "I got you! Hold on, dearest!" Eugene said, grabbing on to her.

Elfriede wrapped her arms tightly around Eugene and held on for dear life. She then looked up for a moment and gave him a kiss on the cheek as a token of her gratitude.

"Elfriede why did you come here… I told you I'd come for you when it was safe. But it seems you had other plans and what on earth where you thinking, bringing your music box," he said, with a grim face.

Elfriede looked down feeling ashamed. "I was worried about you…and I feel safe when I have my music box." She took a deep breath, "But I lost it fighting off that shadow."

Eugene hugged her, "Next time trust me, now you're in the middle of a dangerous situation and that box of yours makes you a target. Probably best for now that it's no longer in your possession."

Seconds later he shouted, "Look out!"

One of the shadows swooped down on top of them and almost knocked them off the chandelier. "Wow! That was close!" he shouted.

Eugene then glanced down and could see that the sword fight still raged on.

He then continued to shift his weight abruptly to swing the chandelier out of harm's way from another attacking shadow. Still on the balcony where Elfriede had left her, Karlotta managed to fly away after Elfriede's escape. Tumbled off on its side, was Elfriede's music box still lying on the floor where she dropped it. One of the shadows finally took notice and swooped down to retrieve it. Marianne saw this too and shouted, "The music box! Bring it here! Bring it to me!"

In a flash her loyal shadow flew over to Marianne and handed her the music box. Her eyes lit up with excitement. She held the music box tightly and immediately could feel the warmth and vibrations that it still emitted. Marianne got a small taste of the euphoric love and magic that the music box was capable of delivering. She then decided to take matters into her own hands. She wasn't quite sure how to harness the powers the music box had locked inside. Remembering some of the sorcery that Adalwolf had taught her, she started to chant in some strange language while holding the music box high above her head. With every passing moment her voice grew louder as she continued her chants. Strange sounds and vibrations began to emit around the music box. A blanket of darkness as black as ink but somehow transparent, slowly enveloped Marianne and surrounded her.

This strange maelstrom of sorcery caught the attention of Elfriede as she continued to swing from the chandelier. Frightened already, Elfriede saw something evil, something of dark sorcery that could harm her and all her friends. Marianne looked like she was moments away from unleashing some sort of dark magic. The look and sounds Elfriede witnessed were downright horrifying. How could this be, she thought. After all she's been through, and losing everything she held dear. This clearly looked like the end as she knew it. Tingles and prickly goosebumps suddenly covered her body. Elfriede began to feel faint and her eyes rolled back into her head. Flash! A flickered vision surrounded her. It was a vision of her dear father, Gustav. How she missed him so much, but strangely felt his presence. Now she could see herself dancing with him and could feel that special love that only a father and daughter could share.

As quickly as this vision appeared, it faded. Her disappointment was so painful. She would never see her dear father again. Elfriede's eyes opened up and she felt a surge of power. An omnipotence she had never felt. She felt no fear but only a sense of courage. And just like that, Elfriede let go of Eugene and leaped toward the balcony. She landed on the railing and leaped one last time focusing only on her music box. As she came crashing down she snatched the music box from Marianne's hands and boom! She hit the floor and tumbled a few yards away. Instantly, the cloud of black sorcery that surrounded Marianne disappeared. The music box was now back in Elfriede's hands and immediately she felt her familiar connection. The one that bonded her and Gustav. Oh, if only Gustav could share their victory. If only they could dance again. If only…

Marianne screamed with contempt and rage, "No!" A swarm of shadows surged toward Elfriede. In a fit of rage, Marianne soon joined the stampede of her shadows as they closed in on Elfriede.

As the approaching dark swarm neared her, Elfriede felt a sense of confidence and security as she held on to her music box. All new vibrations and majestic harmonies now emitted from her music box and grew louder by the second. The same tune that she heard on the battlefield was now audible once more. Elfriede felt at peace and remained calm, she knew everything would be fine. Just as Marianne and her shadows were about to strike, a blast of light and orbs of color erupted from the music box. Bang!...Crack! This fountain of colors and sounds blasted Marianne and her shadows up in the air and slammed them into the castle wall. The shockwave from the blast was so powerful, that it also broke the chain that held up the chandelier. Now Eugene and the chandelier came crashing down toward the floor below. Crash! Crystal and glass shattered all over. Luckily, the chandelier broke Eugene's fall but it tossed him across the room leaving him unconscious.

This was only a few yards away from Adalwolf and General Kristof's sword duel. It startled and broke the concentration of both men. Adalwolf seemed to be distracted even more knowing that above him in the balcony, his queen was injured.

General Kristof could see that Adalwolf clearly lost his concentration, and took advantage of this opportunity. Instinctively, Kristof sprung forward without hesitation and spiraled through the air with a spectacular move. As he came to a landing, he swiftly knocked the sword out of Adalwolf's hand. Then with a final strike, Kristof thrusted his sword into the leg of Adalwolf bringing the king to the ground. Adalwolf let out an almost animalistic growl, mumbling under his breath, "you think you won Kristoff." He reached into his boot revealing a black dagger. Then he raised his hand and sent the dagger flying toward the General,

Eugene realized what Adalwolf was up too and shouted, "Kristoff watch out!"

With lightning fast reflexes and hawk like precision, the General spun around, parrying the hurtling dagger with his sword. Adalwolf began to breathe heavily, gasping for air as he looked up at Kristof. Waiting, still alive and in much pain, groveling before his enemies, Adalwolf only had just enough strength to grab the leg of the victorious Kristof.

"Impossible, impossible…no one defeats me!" Adalwolf wailed.

Teodora, the creatures and Kristof's men all together circled Adalwolf, taking him into their custody. They let out a roar of celebration. The feeling of joy and relief could be felt amongst everyone. The battle had been won, and they came out victorious. General Kristof then stepped away from the injured Adalwolf and made his way over to Eugene who was still lying on the floor… The General looked down upon the lad and spoke to him proudly. "I owe you a debt, you saved my life young man."

"You owe me nothing, it was the right thing to do!" Eugene mumbled between breaths. Eugene reached up to grab the hand offered by Kristof and pulled himself to his feet. He inspected himself for any injuries from the fall, but he appeared unharmed, only his ankle felt sprained.

General Kristoff unsheathed his sword and held it skyward his voice booming, "You all fought valiantly this day and victory is ours!" Then he placed the sword back inside its scabbard.

Everyone cheered for him shouting in unison, "All hail General Kristoff. Promptly, a small group of soldiers dragged Adalwolf off to the far end of the foyer where his queen Marianne now waited. Briefly, the two of them looked into each other's eyes, but nothing was said. Adalwolf, his queen and the few remaining shadows, huddled together in unity as they pondered their future. Seconds later, Kristof's men surrounded the group and took them off to be locked away deep inside the castle dungeon.

The Waltz and Ending

Once back on his feet, Eugene dusted himself off and made his way over to the grand staircase. He began to race up the stairs skipping a few steps at a time making his way toward Elfriede. Still a little shaken, Elfriede dashed over to the top of the steps meeting Eugene as he arrived. She jumped up into the loving arms of Eugene wrapping her legs around his waist and gave him the biggest hug. The two of them remained in this position for a few minutes as the both rocked back and forth slowly. For the first time in days, Elfriede felt safe and secure.

Eugene asked, "Are you alright my love?"

"Yes, dear… I'm OK," she cried. "When you fell…I thought I lost you for good."

Eugene looked her deep in the eyes. "You won't get rid of me that easily," he said laughing to himself.

They both giggled and Eugene gave her such a big hug that he swept her right off of her feet.

The two of them then made their way down the long flight of stairs and down to the grand foyer.

Down below the crowd waited, everyone was smiling and hugs were shared. Karlotta had the biggest smile of all as she embraced Elfriede, holding her tight. The two of them shared a few laughs just like they did when they first met. Then with her jolly but stern voice, Karlotta piped up and loudly announced, "This calls for a celebration! Shall we dance? Off to the ballroom!"

The crowd gathered together as Karlotta led them into the grand ballroom which was located off the foyer. The group made its way into the ballroom and then paused. The room was dimly lit, with only a few candles flickering behind some glass sconces that hung on the wall. With a playful grin, Karlotta gestured toward Teodora grabbing her attention. Teodora knew exactly what Karlotta was thinking. She smiled back before turning around to face her family of creatures. Like a conductor, she slowly raised her hands up in the air and then lowered them. Then in unity, that harmony of voices filled the air and surrounded everyone. Moments later, the grand chandeliers that hung high above, began to magically glow and twinkle with light. The crowd other than the creatures, were taken back and caught up in the moment. Elfriede and Eugene were separated from the crowd standing in the center of the ballroom gazing up at the spectacle.

"Wow, how beautiful...how magical this is," Elfriede whispered.

Yet, never before had Elfriede felt such a mixture of emotions. The joy of reuniting with Eugene, the joy of freeing the world from the evil sorcery, the victory of her friends, yet the longing, the pain of the loss of Gustav hurt so much, the potion that once numbed her of such sorrows was no longer active. Never again would they dance together. Never again would she feel that paternal love that was like no other.

Teodora stood looking at Elfriede and Eugene and saw the love between them. She slowly waved her hand once more in the direction of the two lovers. Softly, the sweet sound of violins filled the air. It was the most beautiful composition that Elfriede could ever recall. Her eyes became glazed and her heart started pumping. Instinctively, Eugene gently grabbed Elfriede's right hand and then wrapped his left arm around her waist.

The sweet song of the violins continued and the melody repeated itself in 3/4 time. The tempo was slow, and the two of them gently glided into a romantic waltz. Teodora, and the entire group gathered together forming a circle around the lovely couple and watched with glee. This was a special moment for Elfriede and Eugene, and for them only. As the two of them cascaded around the ballroom floor, Elfriede never took her eyes off Eugene. She starred deeply into his eyes and could only smile. A few minutes later, the tempo of the music picked up. One by one, the group of onlookers paired up with one another and joined the couple on the dance floor. Soldiers and all, it was a spectacle to see, a joyous celebration. The lights above shimmered and a golden aura of light lit up the ballroom. Eventually the sound of the music came to an end. Elfriede and Eugene were the last couple that remained dancing. They were now dancing at a slower pace, and each of them continued to gaze into each other's eyes. Eugene then noticed Elfriede bite her lip slightly as tears pooled in the corner of her eyes.

"What's wrong my love? Why are you sad?" he asked.

Elfriede began to openly cry and sniffle out a few sentences. "My father. How I miss him so much. I can never forget the times we danced together as father and daughter. That was my life. How we connected…what made me feel whole and complete.

"My dear, the love I feel for you is real and as pure as it gets… but I can never replace the loss of your father."

"As we danced together this evening, I soon found myself thinking of him." Elfriede said.

Elfriede now sobbed profoundly as she rested her head into Eugene's chest. Eugene remained quiet for a moment, but then spoke up. "My dear Elfriede, your father will be with you always…I know this. Remember to keep him in your heart, and he will always be there."

Elfriede nodded her head briefly in agreement, then let go of Eugene and slowly walked away. Eugene's head dropped in the ultimate sadness for his lover's loss. Now standing there alone, he could only look down at the ground and reflect for a moment. He remembered that bond between them. They truly were close, and they both shared such an intense passion for music and dance.

Elfriede continued to walk away and out of the ballroom. She walked a few yards down the empty hallway and over to a frost-covered window. The window looked out into the barren countryside now lit up by the moon. She reached out with her hand and touched the glass. It was cold, and she could see her breath collect in a slow moving mist as she pressed her face even closer. She looked again up at the moon and began to tremble slightly. The flood of emotions was clearly taking over and her heart began to race. Her father, the music and dance were now just a memory. Elfriede felt cold, confused and lost. Then suddenly, the warmth of someone's hand gently caressed the back of her arm. Startled, Elfriede spun around to see who it was. There smiling up at her, was the beautiful Teodora. She grabbed a hold of Elfriede's hand and said, "For all that you have lost...there is so much more that you have given. It was you and your sacrifice, that have made the difference. Now there is peace for everyone across these lands...Your kindness and love have made this all possible. Remember, dear, it was your father who gave you that music box, and it was the music box that sought out you. Together you connected...connected in the most magical way. Your music box will continue to bring you happiness, and re-live those special times with your father."

For a brief moment Elfriede smiled.

She slowly bent down and kissed Teodora softly on the cheek. As she rose back up, she turned and continued to look out the window once again. Teodora let out a deep breath and walked away slowly. As she made her way back into the ballroom, she approached Karlotta who was all alone.

Karlotta noticed a strange look on Teodora's face. "What is it, Teodora?" she asked softly. The two of them began to have a few words and finished off with a long embrace. They hugged for a few more moments, then parted. Teodora continued into the ballroom, heading over to her group of creatures.

Karlotta proceeded in the opposite direction walking over toward Elfriede. When she reached Elfriede, she stopped, held out her hand and said, "Come with me, dear." Elfriede turned around and didn't know what to say. But she trusted Karlotta like a sister, and grabbed her hand. Karlotta then led the way back into the ballroom with Elfriede following close behind.

As they entered the grand ballroom, the first thing Elfriede noticed was General Kristof's army. He had all his soldiers lined up in formation facing one direction. Then she began to hear that glorious familiar sound of music. It was that beautiful harmony sung together amongst the creatures. Again, the creatures were banded together in a large circle performing some sort of ritual, but why, Elfriede wondered. Swirls of colors and sparkling mist filled the air as Karlotta led Elfriede toward the creatures. It was beautifully choreographed as the winged creatures paired up together spinning around with each other. The smaller creatures seemed to be intertwined, weaving in and out with the rest of the group as the circle they formed started to grow. Magical, very magical, but where was Teodora, Elfriede thought. Like before, the musical vibrations and chants picked up and became louder with each passing moment. But for some strange reason, the sound and theme of this ritual was unsettling for Elfriede. There was something a little different about this and Elfriede started to feel uneasy.

Suddenly, a loud pop filled the room as a light flashed brilliantly from the center of the circle. Following the explosion of light, the creatures could be heard crying out a sigh of relief and resolution. Elfriede then witnessed a brief look of sadness on some of the creature's faces. But that only lasted a moment, and soon many of the creatures began to smile again. There was a sense of joy and much love that emanated from the entire group. The sound of music and uncharted vibrations was clearly very different than anything Elfriede had ever experienced before. It had the angelic feeling of pure love.

Still guided by Karlotta, Elfriede now found herself caught up inside the creatures' circle. One by one, the creatures seemed to hand off Elfriede as she glided her way through the ever-growing circle. Soon the winged creatures took over, wrapping their glorious wings around Elfriede's body spinning her around in opposite directions. Elfriede could see nothing, only the closed-in darkness that surrounded her inside the confines of her winged host. Outside she could still hear the chants and glorious music that continued to grow louder. Elfriede spun slowly a few more times and came to a stop as the last winged creature opened up her wings and released her.

The vibrations, chants and music suddenly stopped. Elfriede now found herself in the center of the circle standing alone. Her body began to tingle and a sense of euphoria swept over her. Then slowly, one last creature spun around and passed in front of Elfriede. The winged creature stopped and faced her. The creature stood there silently and held its wings closed. Small sparks of light popped and danced all around its body. Then slowly, the creature lifted up its wings to reveal what she had concealed. Through the smoke and some magical mist, Elfriede found herself looking at a familiar face. She dropped to her knees and began to cry. Her hands covered her face as she fought off the tears of joy. Then in a moment of magic, she felt the loving arms of her father reach down and pick her up! Gustav held his daughter tightly and raised her high in the air. Immediately, Elfriede wrapped her arms around her father's neck and pressed her face against his as she continued to sob. Elfriede's body began to shake and tears started to stream down her face. She cried out, "Father....Father! Is it a dream?"

Gustav then said, "I'm here, my love...somehow and someway... I'm here!" The sound of her father's voice was the only thing Elfriede wanted to hear.

General Kristof, his men and all the creatures were now in a group that surrounded Elfriede and her father. The crowd around them began clapping, and let out a joyous roar. There were smiles everywhere, and you could feel the love that filled the room. Elfriede let go of her father and walked over to Karlotta and gave her a big hug. She knew something was different, the look on Karlotta's face told here everything.

"Where is she?" Elfriede asked. "Where is Teodora?"

Karlotta then said, "She is with us, dear. She is part of us all now."

Elfriede looked on as Karlotta continued to explain. "Teodora was the strongest of all us creatures. She was the only one that held a special but powerful gift. The gift of life itself. But this magic comes with a cost a life for a life. The only way to bring back your father, dear, was to say goodbye and crossover. She loved you so much and was very proud of what you gave to others. This was her way of giving you back the love that you lost. This powerful magic can only work when used on someone special, someone that is pure of heart, who has the innocence of a child, loves music and cares deeply for others. Remember, the music box connected with you, only you my dear Elfriede."

The moment felt bittersweet and Elfriede knew what was done, could not be undone. It was the most beautiful thing someone could do to make someone else happy. Elfriede then reached out and took both hands of Karlotta, holding them tightly. With slight tears in her eyes, she could only grin after feeling mixed emotions about everything. Karlotta said nothing but returned a cheerful smile. Elfriede walked back over to her father where he was waiting patiently. Gustav smiled widely and opened his arms once again to hold his daughter. As the two embraced, Elfriede felt a soft tickle on her face. Her eyes lit up for a moment with excitement. "Teodora….is that you?" Elfriede looked up at the grand chandelier where she saw a little spark of light that twinkled for a moment and then disappeared.

Elfriede smiled, offered a wink and whispered just two words. "Thank you."

A Familiar Voice

Hieke closed the book thinking to herself what a wonderful ending it had, there was a lot of tragedy but overall she felt things balanced out and she loved books with happy endings. No sooner than she stood up to put the book back on its shelf, she heard her Oma calling.

"Hieke dinner is ready, don't make your Opa wait."

She placed the book back beside the music box and giggled to herself. She couldn't get over how real it felt while reading the story. She swore that she could almost smell the smoke from the Shadows and whenever Elfriede felt sad or happy she did as well. She shook it off as her imagination playing tricks on her and started dancing out of the library pretending she was her favorite character Elfriede. Half way out of the library she heard a loud thud, which stooped her dead in her tracks. What was that she thought to herself. She turned around examining her surroundings. Then she heard her Oma calling once more.

"Hieke dinner is getting cold, come down stairs and join us."

With haste she made her way to the door, but again she stopped. This time the lights dimmed and started flashing.

"Is someone there?" Hieke said.

Then she heard a faint ghastly voice, it rang in her ears. Strangely she recognized it as Teodora. "Teodora is that you?" She said aloud, rationalizing why she would even ask such a silly question, as it was impossible for a character of a story to be here, in the flesh in her Oma's library.

"Elfriede your friends need you." The voice echoed.

Once again the lights flickered on and off and this time she saw a small spark whisk through the air, heading back to her favorite cubbyhole. Fueled with curiosity she went to examine the phenomenon. As Hieke neared the cubby she noticed a book on the floor, its cover was facing up. She walked over and picked up the book, it had the same exact leather binding as the previous one. So, she glanced at the bookshelf to make sure it didn't fall down and to her surprise the book was still there, perfectly intact.

She dusted off its cover and the title had a faint glow. She slowly traced her finger over the letters one by one and said out loud, "RETURN TO THE FERN BLACKWOOD'S"

Hieke flipped it open to the first page and noticed that it was blank, she flipped through the book feverishly taking note that all of the pages were blank. Then she went back to the first page once more and gold lettering began to dance around the page, and materialized into several paragraphs. Her jaw went slack as she watched in amazement, she was at a loss for words. How is this possible she thought to herself?

She started reading the opening paragraph, "Elfriede danced around the castles ballroom with her father. Today was a joyous day for her and she was bubbling over with joy, she could not wait to go visit her friends in the Fern Blackwood's and share her great news, especially with her best friend Karlotta. She had not visited her friends in several weeks and missed them very much."

The sound of her Oma coming up the stairs jarred Hieke. She quickly picked up her blanket and tucked the book safely away. This book was magical and she feared that her Oma would not let her have it, especially if she discovered its true nature.

Hieke leaned down to the book and whispered, "Teodora…I know that it was your voice I heard. Don't worry I'll be back to read what your trying to share with me."

She then ran over to the door and greeted her Oma.

"You always get lost in your books Hieke. You need to make friends, is not good to spend all your vacation in library reading. Your Opa got tired of waiting and started eating his dinner without you," her Oma said.

Heike slouched her shoulders and then said, "I'm sorry Oma. You know that I am shy and have a hard time getting along with kids my age."

Heike flipped the light switch and shut the door behind her. The book literally had her entranced as her mind raced about what she discovered. She could not wait to examine the book further and figure out how it worked. She never seen anything like it, the book was way too old be electronic, and she never saw anything remotely similar to what she just witnessed. There was no way for her to explain how this was possible. Pages of books don't just come alive; it just doesn't work that way. Her final thought was that it had to be magic, there was no other explanation and she could not wait to visit the library again and see if Teodora would make contact with her.

If you are not currently following Ron Kramer and would like to follow him on social media, join his mailing list for free gifts and upcoming title notifications...then visit his website today **http://www.musicboxstory.com** for more details.